Feminist on Fire

A Novel

Coleen Kearon

Fomite
Burlington, Vermont

ISBN-13: 978-1-942515-24-1
Library of Congress Control Number: 2015947756

Fomite
58 Peru Street
Burlington, VT 05401
www.fomitepress.com

Author photo: Durwood Mark Collier
Cover art—*Urban Girl*, mixed media
© 2015 Dominique Gustin
https://www.etsy.com/people/dominiquegustin

Pam Kearon

1943-2010

And for my sister, Dawn, whose unsurpassed humor and compassion I'm honored to share in on a daily basis.

Many thanks to Susannah Noel, my accomplished and attentive copy editor; Christopher Noel, a most astute and generous reader; to my writing group, Kathryn Guare, Susan Ritz, and Shelagh Shapiro; and finally, to all of those whose work has inspired me along the way: Rebecca Williams, Erlene Hendrix, Tom Heath, Brit-Maike L. Garland, Jennifer McMahon, Paul Gartski, Tippi, Mark Doty, and Donna Bister and Marc Estrin of Fomite Press.

"There are always two deaths, the real one and the one people
know about."
—Jean Rhys, *Wide Sargasso Sea*

"A thinking woman sleeps with monsters
that beak which grips her, she becomes."
—Adrienne Rich

Contents

No More

I WAKE UP FEELING LIKE I've been propelled from the ocean, slapped on a deserted, bone-colored shore. My mouth is dry, eyes sandy. Cracking them, from my sideways position, I am faced with the small, dung-colored refrigerator that my father bought me, and a roach's antenna, spangling wildly, its backside or a leg or something caught in the ice that has gummed up around the miniature door. Crumbs of food are embedded in the opaque, vaguely stinking slick.

My friend Ida came over about six months ago and filled each orifice in the walls and floors with steel wool, so that it appeared that I had aged pubic hair sprouting here and there. Tao, my cat, strikes at the tight coils, so they now hang half in, half out, allowing ample room for the roaches' passage. Ida also told me to wrap the toothpaste and my brush in tinfoil, which I did for a few days after she left. But I started to forget and then forgot altogether.

The sounds in the hallway are both faint and carrying. People in and out, checking their mail, coming in from buying cigarettes or a slice or a bagel. I turn and face the wall, disturbing the sour smells of the bed and my body. A deep crack, like an artery, bubbles up from under the flaking paint. Something about looking at it makes me think about how hungry I am but how I don't want to move.

Someone has laid a finger on one of the buzzers. The super threatens from the third-floor window. The whining stops.

My father is coming over today to take my laundry. He comes each Saturday to collect my filthy clothes and sheets, clean my apartment, and buy me food. He provides services and supplies. I think he performs these many tasks because he loves me in a way, feels guilty in another way, and ashamed, in yet another way. He wouldn't want anyone else to see me as I am, even a paid, professional stranger. My father thinks I am his secret, though that is hardly the case. The police have been here. The super prays for a reason to evict me. He's told me that, jabbing his finger in my face. He keeps his eyes and ears open. The family all know about me. But that's different. My father and mother have long stopped talking to their respective families. She sits at the kitchen table, smokes and drinks coffee from the moment she rises until she reaches the other end of the day. The television is usually on, but mostly she stares out the window into the small, concrete backyard, guarded by a cheap metal fence and back to back with other cheap metal fences, the row house fences of Canarsie, Brooklyn. My mother rarely changes out of her housedress, a thin thing with snaps along the front and a pattern of acorns? Pine needles? Something like that. Homey, and not at all consonant with my mother. At eleven, she downs the burnt swill from the bottom of the Mr. Coffee decanter, and her short, brittle legs bow on their way up the dark stairway to the second floor. My father cleans their house, too. Often, he is still cleaning when she goes to bed. He does all the wash, mops, scours floors and sinks and toilets. She won't lift a finger, but runs him, calling at him from her perch in the kitchen or in her bed, "Howard!" All day, he drinks beer in the basement, shuffling up and down the basement steps and around the house while he does the housework. Not drunk, but blurred. His sense of hearing diminished, I sure hope, so as to hear her voice only at a great distance, from down a corridor and around a bend or under something very large and pillowy. He's an old man now, in his late sixties. He no longer stands up to my mother, not that he ever did in any effective way. But he used to make some sort of show at bucking her. Talking back. But that was long ago, when they were both still young and before his breath fogged the good silver, a knife raised to within inches of his nose and mouth. My mother genuinely frightens people. She could've given murderous despots like Hitler and Stalin a lifetime of shit and regret. Her power runs deep. It is unquestioned by me and my father. And everyone who has ever challenged her has been banished. Like the two families my mother and father won't acknowledge exist any longer, hers and his. No more.

A loud knocking bleeds through the many layers of my head, pounding, pounding. My dad calls me Pammy, short for Pamela.

"Pammy, Pammy, it's me. Open up."

My father is here; it is no longer morning. My eyes tear open. Sore. My throat is sore, too. So dry. I'm on the bone-colored shore again, tossed there like a length of seaweed or an empty shell. For days and days, I have slept. Tao screams and paces at the sound of my father's voice. There will be food. His box will be cleaned. He will feel restored.

"Okay," I yell. "Hang on a minute."

I sit up. I'm so much fatter than I used to be, even a year ago. Two years. It's the medications, they say. And not moving. Sleeping forever and ever, buried under days and days, passing near eye-level, in subwaylike windows, far underground.

Reveille

Next to the small bathroom sink there is a giant bottle of Jergens hand lotion. It is shaped like a tear, and the smell clings to not only the bathroom air, but all the air on the second floor, because my mother has a bottle in her room, too. The smell is sharp, its white the white of buried silence.

The sink is blue. It matches the blue of the blue-and-black floor tile. There is a small window way up above the tub. Long and very narrow. There is no sun this morning, so everything inside looks flat. My nightdress is hiked up and the floor is cold against my legs and feet. Drops of water the size of pinpricks sweat on the exposed plumbing.

It is early, before my parents have gotten up, but they are awake. I can hear them laughing. This is what they do on weekend mornings. Soon my father will come in to use the bathroom. If he catches me before I've had a chance to get back to my room, he will ask if I slept in here, angrily. He'll say it's silly and I'll catch a draft. When I say nothing, but scooch closer to the toilet, he will yank at my arm and tell me to stop it now. He speaks softly, so my mother won't hear him. But sometimes she catches the edge of his whispering voice, and yells from the bed. We both listen and watch for her to arrive from down the dark, narrow hallway and into the small bathroom entrance, leading with her chest. She knocks my father out of the way and grabs me by the hair. When she pulls my hair out, the pain is like a burn and it lasts for days. Once, when it was right in the front, my father kept me home from school for three days, and he took off work. My mother said, "Do what you want. I'm going to work," and we sat together in the kitchen and he sang to me, "Ireland Must Be Heaven Because My Mother was Born There." He gave me a fireman's carry up and down the basement stairs while he washed the clothes.

My father and I don't talk about the hair or the bathroom. He used to ask me more about why I slept in there; now, he just tells me not to. I know the nights when my mother is going to come into my room. Earlier, downstairs, there's something about the way she tells me to go up and get ready now, her eyes maybe. When I'm not in my room, she goes back to bed, like she forgot what she was going to say. But if I'm there, the door cracks open and shut. She stands in the dark, whispering, so that my father won't hear her, just like he doesn't want her to hear him. But I have to listen. She will kill the three of us one night, but she won't say which one, with gas or knives. The smell of hand cream sticks in my nose and throat.

THE LAUGHTER HAS JUST STOPPED. I crawl from under the toilet and make it back to my room in time to miss my father. My room which feels like an empty icebox. I pull the covers up over my head and breathe in my own warm breath. I will be seven years old next week, on December second. I'm in the third grade because I skipped a grade. Miss Hargrave is my teacher at St. John's. She has long brown hair parted in the middle and she is younger than most of the other teachers. Last week, when I couldn't fall asleep after recess, she lifted me onto her lap and read to me. Before I went home, I wrote her a letter about how I loved her and she smiled and said I was sweet and so smart. "So different for your age," she said. She showed me a picture of her cat, Harry, and said maybe I could meet him sometime. "We live near each other. I'm on E. 93rd Street, just a block away." I wish I could go live with Ms. Hargrave. Her boyfriend has long hair and he smiles a lot. They wave from across the street sometimes, when they're on their way for a slice and I'm in the front yard. I watch them until they go into the pizzeria, my hands and part of my arms reaching through the fence.

"*Reveille, reveille,* all hands on deck," my father yells down the hallway. "The smoking lamp is now lit." My father was in the Navy for four years. He went to India and my mother had to go live with her mother. I wasn't born then but my sister Carol and my brother Charlie were. My mother got sick and the family had to take care of them for a long time. My sister said that my grandmother made a big dinner every Sunday and the whole family came and helped. They drank beer and talked until it was late, like they never wanted to leave. There were twelve brothers and sisters. Some of them have died now, and we don't see the rest of the family anymore. When my father talks about being in the Navy and in India, I can tell he didn't want to come home.

Remember How This Feels

From the speaker platform I have a slight aerial view of the crowd. Hundreds of women reach farther back than my eye can see, chanting "ABORTION RIGHTS NOW!"

It is so fucking cold, a late October Saturday. My breath is visible. We had planned the protest for early September, but the city, the city being fucking white men, kept finding ways to hold up our permits.

I must've walked up here. Arrived at this spot somehow, only a moment ago. But I don't remember the walk, the arrival. All blank! The chant continues and I smile at the faces I cannot see. My first line bobs up to the surface of my brain, like a buoy.

I say, "There is evidence that pre-historic societies were matriarchal." The crowd goes wild. The force of hundreds of people stomping their feet rattles the podium. Someone screams, 'The first sex,' managing to be heard above the ambient roar, and hundreds of fists break into the air. I continue, my voice rising to be heard above the hoots. My eyes contact other women's eyes, looking into them. I feel the crowd listening, and my hands and arms wave, like a conductor. "Cave paintings of pregnant women suggest that men didn't realize they were in part responsible for pregnancy, and that pregnant women were worshiped because they had the sole power to create life. Women historians conjecture that it was when men realized their part in pregnancy that the patriarch rose in order to control women's bodies." I point accusingly, my voice as strong and loud as it has ever been. "Their opposition to safe, legal abortions is one of the various means by which men enslave women, along with the institution of marriage, the dictates of religion that define women solely as wives and mothers, the threat and the practice of rape, the pathologizing and shunning of women who seek sexual gratification, not to mention the unimaginably violent practices against our sisters in other cultures." I begin naming, the words incantations: "Chinese foot binding, African and Mid-Eastern cliterodectomies, and the stoning and burning to death women suspected of adultery. It is our charge to free all women of a patriarch that mutilates women's bodies and souls; a patriarch that isolates women from each other by prostituting them into marriage, and one that inculcates female children to reflect men's image of women as virgins or whores, their bodies targeted for rape and murder." I pause. I look at the front row and slowly let my eyes travel to the outermost reaches of the crowd: "It is our charge to reclaim and resurrect the matriarch, to fashion a new world in which females and their children live without fear, without oppression, fully realizing our power as women to forge our own destiny. The right to safe and legal abortion will be a giant step for womankind, and a killing blow that the patriarch so richly deserves."

I do not say that my mother did not want to be a mother and I did not want to be born of her: *this is the bond we share.* There is shame in this thought, regardless of its truth.

The applause is so loud I stop for a moment. Police officers stand on the outskirts of the park, trying to appear disinterested, but with billy clubs dangling from their hips. Fuck them. Fuck the brims of their hats that cover their eyes so that all you see are the quick dashes of their disapproving mouths.

I turn slightly to look at the panel seated behind the podium. Susan Brownmiller rises and walks toward me in two long strides, her short wavy brown hair contained under a crocheted hat. I am told we resemble each other. Our facial features, anyway. Wavy black hair, brown eyes, prominent, but not large, noses. Her movement is much more assured and graceful than my earth-bound shuffle, my feet like weights. Clapping, Susan places her left hand on my shoulder, and leans toward the microphone, coming whisper close to the side of my face. Yelling above the sounds of the audience, she thanks me, and talks about how *The Feminists* are helping redefine the Women's Movement, adding a fresh and vital perspective to the feminist discourse that is both intellectually and emotionally rigorous. The back of my legs burn with the cold as I take my seat again.

Susan introduces Bella Abzug. The police look less indifferent at the sound of Bella's name. Their postures uniformly stiffen, like cardboard, the billy clubs shifting in their holsters. The audience screams and hoots their welcome. They know Bella. Or of her. I was a total surprise. And I surprised myself in front of these two hundred or so people. I didn't think I could go through with it today, though I desperately wanted it to go well. Despite the vodka and valium breakfast, my mind did not settle until I started speaking. Then, I felt what the words I'd written and practiced for days and days were saying. I didn't think about or even hear them as they were being spoken. It was like forgetting myself. A gift, that.

Bella says, "I'm running for President, and I cannot do it alone!" She pumps her fist in the air. A seeming universal gesture for the fight we are all poised to join. She points into the crowd, "We will do this. Each and every one of us standing here today."

With everyone else on the panel, I stand and clap along with the audience until my palms hurt. The metronome sound of so many hands keeping time is tribal. I look at the back of Bella's head, at one of her signature wide brimmed hats, and at the stone cold air. For the first time since the symposium started, I see Barbara in the audience. She waves and I smile.

I realize that I am not in the flat and airless space I normally occupy. I tell myself to remember how this feels. I wonder if other people feel this way in general, more integrated with people and space and time, less abstract. It would explain why most people don't wonder if they should kill themselves every day. Ha, ha.

I've been writing and giving most of the speeches for *The Feminists* for the past two months, ever since I gave an impromptu speech at the Vanguard one night. A Village Voice reporter was there and the next week, he wrote about my inebriated eloquence and sharp oratory. High as I was, I remember little but the lights from the bar glinting over the top of peoples' heads and how their attention followed me in each thought I had. It felt like change was no longer being talked or thought about, but happening at that very moment, that we had finally come together to do good. Maybe I have a chance in this world that is nothing like my mother's.

SUSAN IS AT THE PODIUM again, introducing the next speaker. It begins to drizzle; fine threads twist in the air like those barber shop signs. Everyone was told to dress warmly and to bring umbrellas, which now whump open. Hundreds of roosting crows spill into the sky from a nearby tree.

The Afro-American woman I was introduced to when I first arrived addresses the crowd. "My name is Rebecca Street." She is a tall woman, around 5"10, her umbrella held high as she leans in and down, adjusting the microphone.

I know how we black and white and brown and yellow sisters like to come together when we're tearing down the men. But it seems to me that when we're asked to look at class and race issues among women," Rebecca Street pauses here and looks at the audience before continuing, "when we are asked to address class and color in the very movement that aims to end women's oppression, we fall silent. And we fall apart. Like the Black Power Movement, the Women's Movement marginalizes women of color and poor women. This has to change. It's time to embrace women other than white, college educated ones. I agree that the right to abortion is the legal fight we need to wage and to win. However, we have economic and social battles that also must be organized in order to provide all women with choice, not only over their bodies, but over their lives."

The spiraling drizzle picks up and people shuffle in discomfort. When they realize her speech has ended, the applause begins. The panel stands and the applause takes on new momentum. The crows have returned, and fill the air not only with their black forms, but with their cries.

Falling hard and sideways, the rain begins in earnest.

"It's nice to be here, and nice to be asked," Rebecca Street says. "You are invited and encouraged to attend meetings of the Black Women's Coalition to end Racism, Classism, and Sexism," she yells. "We meet at the Y on 42nd Street on Mondays, Wednesdays, and Fridays at 5 pm."

The crowd quickly disperses. Susan and I hug. "Are you coming to the restaurant?" she asks.

"I'll meet you there. I need stop by my apartment first," I yell, to be heard through the noise of the pelting rain.

Barbara steps onto the stage, her jeans and blouse soaked through. "Great job," she says. "Really."

Her warm hazel eyes smile at me. I tell her about lunch. "I can't," she says. "I wish I could, but I have so much grading to do, you wouldn't believe it."

In my disappointment, I look away. Smiling, I say: "Thanks for coming. I know you're busy."

I manage to catch Rebecca before she leaves. I touch her arm and say, "Thank you."

"Don't thank me," she says, looking me in the eye. "Come to our meetings. Change the color of this movement, sister."

I say I will, and I mean to try. But I know I am afraid of black women, of their frank stares on the trains, as if they can see the fear in my heart. There are no black women in the meetings we organize and attend, just the ones on the subway. Rebecca Street is right.

Within a few minutes pretty much everyone is gone, head first and under their umbrellas, trying to shield their faces from the driving rain. I watch the police walk to their cars in their glossy black slickers, and a couple of volunteers dismantle and load the makeshift stage, the podium and the microphone, into a van. My cheap umbrella webs in and out in the wind.

I move under a tree, its leaves swept vertical. My hand finds my bottle in the large, dark satchel I've slung around my neck. The Matriarch may not rise again in my lifetime, but we are laying the groundwork. I can feel the world changing; we all can.

Above the crows soar and land in the high tree branches. Vodka hums inside me. I can't go to lunch. Don't want to go. I want to lie down. The rain slaps against the pavement and the leaves look like they're hanging on for their lives. What if the rain and the wind just never stopped, washing away the sins of the world? Walking, I look back. The birds' black bodies converge in the bare tree branches, so quiet, you might miss them if you didn't already know they were there.

Dad Is the Same Way

Dear Charlie,

We got your letter from Dunoon, Scotland yesterday. It sounds beautiful there. I plan to look it up next time I'm at the library. I can't stop thinking about you living mostly on a submarine, how you must feel and think like a fish moving through the depths. What a long way from Brooklyn you are in every way.

I hope you get this letter. Daddy said people don't always receive their mail when they're overseas, and you could be stationed somewhere else by the time this gets to Scotland, but I thought I would still try to reach you.

I want to ask if you could come home the next time you are on leave. I need your help, and hope that you can arrange for me to go and live with Aunt Mary and Uncle George. I'm pretty certain they would take me. Aunt Mary is so nice to me whenever I see her, and they have such a big house. I get along well with cousin David and the twins. I must get out of here.

The reason is I am afraid of Ma. Dad is the same way. I think he pretends he can't hear the things she says to me. He sings and constantly cleans the house. He barely ever sits down, in fact, and must find in the incessant movement cover from her threats and insults.

Last week, Ma told me that she gave birth to me and that she has the right to kill me if she wants. We were walking out the front door for a doctor's appointment, and she kept shoving me so that I tripped down the porch stairs. I know Daddy saw, because I caught his eye from the living room window. He looked like a ghost standing there behind the sheers. Last night, I heard her tell Daddy that she is going to commit me to the State Hospital. She knew I could hear her. I could rot in someplace like that for all she cares. I have never done anything to Ma, and I don't know why she hates me so much. But she has since I can remember. This is not the first time she has mentioned killing me. Was she like this with you and Carol? I'm beginning to think she must have been.

After Aunt Katherine had a heart attack last Christmas, Daddy and I went to see her in the hospital. She asked about you and Carol. Daddy told her that Carol was doing well in the convent, going to college, and that you were also taking college courses and traveling all over the world in the Navy. When Daddy left to get coffee, Katherine said to Uncle John that it was sad that you both left home so early. Something in her voice made me wonder if you and Carol left because of Ma, and if Aunt Katherine and Uncle John knew about mom. They grew up with her after all. Mom never went to see Katherine. She didn't even call her to ask how she was. I remember how Carol told me Ma got sick when Daddy was in the Navy, and how Grandma had to take care of you both. Do you know if she had a nervous breakdown? Do you remember what happened? I'm writing to Carol, too, but I have even less confidence that she will get my letter. She told me she knows that the boy she met when she was studying at Oxford has written to her, but that she hasn't received a single letter. She thinks the nuns must have been told about him by her English sponsor, and that they've thrown any letters away.

We don't see much of Carol. When she visits she gets drunk on wine and Daddy puts her in a taxi back to Queens right after dinner. A couple of times it has been quite a scene, with her habit getting caught in the car door, and Daddy having to open and close it a number of times before he gets her fully in. On her last visit she yelled from inside the cab about how she practically raised me, and how Ma had always favored you. You know everyone on the block must have been craning their necks to get a look at her. Ma hardly talks to her when she's here. But afterward, she calls her a phony and says how no one ever liked her. She says she doesn't know how she got daughters like us. But Carol is right, you, Ma adores. She and Daddy fight all the time about how he encouraged you to go into the Navy when you could've taken the scholarship at Brooklyn Tech. She hates that you are not here. The Thanksgiving after you left, she told Daddy it was all his fault, and hit him so hard on the side of his head that he started bleeding from his ear. She just sat there while he bled all over the dining room table. She lit a cigarette, and I went and got a dish towel. She is not a normal person. She is dangerous.

I feel that soon I will either be dead or in the State Hospital. She might listen to you if you told her that I had to go live with

Mary and George. You could say it was just for a little while. Maybe we could even get Aunt Katherine or Aunt Mary or somebody to tell her that she needs to rest. I know one thing, if I ever get out of here I will never come home again. The desire never to have been born is strong in me, and getting more so each minute. I cannot live like this anymore, the pain is too great. I know I only have two years of high school remaining, but I feel that it is imperative I leave here now. Please write back as soon as you get this, and let me know if you can help me.

Love, Pammy

So High

Inside, the fire escape steps fall in perfect shadow, ascending the wall nearest the window we just climbed through, to the living room ceiling. We chose the full moon for the light, and once our eyes adjust to the black air, we can see well enough not to bump into the furniture as we crawl through the living room on our hands and knees. Harold is up front. The refrigerator jolts on and off and my heart leaps along with its distinctive bump and shudder. Not only the couple in the master bedroom, way down at the end of the hallway, but the entire Fifth Avenue apartment, which consists of an entire floor, seems in a deep sleep, as if rendered that way to allow our passage.

When we reach the foyer, Harold stands. I remain on all fours, my eyes fastened on the bedroom door. He slides open the hall closet and takes out a mink coat, drapes it over his shoulders. He smiles at me, and nods over to the kitchen. I crawl over, not confident enough to stand upright. Once Harold is inside an apartment or a house, he usually walks around totally unabashed, like he owns the place.

Stainless steel appliances and granite countertops: pools of dark, silvery water, glint in the pale light. Ice cubes tumble and fall through a chute in the refrigerator. It has cleverly concealed handles and a shining surface that looks like the newly waxed floors of television commercials. It is a calm little hub, this kitchen, somewhere you'd come to rest or to die. A shimmering hearth. *Mine eyes have seen the glory.*

We'd smoked a little hash earlier, chased it with vodka so clear I could see the specks of gold that flower around Harold's iris feather kaleidoscopically through the bottom of the glass. The silky vodka welcomes me, its warm embrace definite, fated.

Harold has been here before, invited that time, a friend of a friend who knew this pair of rich people. Trust funds and faraway travels. A Kenyan safari, the Kyoto Gardens. Harold had seen a flash of the coat as the maid opened and closed the closet to hang someone's leather jacket. Harold wasn't wearing a coat that night or now. He doesn't own one. Harold is a beggar, which is how he makes his living, he explains to anyone who listens. He gets up at seven in the morning, just like everyone else, and panhandles during morning rush hour, again at lunch, then at five. He makes about fifteen dollars a day. Sometimes he pretends he is blind. Other times, a Vietnam Vet. It is work! he says mock-playfully, daring anyone to disagree. People laugh but don't think it's funny. He smells and is dirty. I guess that something about his willingness to inflict his stink on anyone within a few feet keeps people in line. I can imagine him on the night he was invited here, insisting on the inferiority of ease, accusing its inhabitants, their cleanliness like cowardice. Harold is young and handsome and he interests affluent young and handsome college boys who've read Genet and Sartre and Dostoevsky. They stand next to him with a Scotch in hand, drinking in his stench, they feel brave and self-congratulatory.

This is our fourth break-in. Harold has met the people whose homes we crawl around in. Usually, we don't touch anything. Like art for art's sake, we break in just because. But from the minute Harold saw the mink, he had plans. He lays it on the kitchen floor, fur side up, takes his dirty clothes off, striptease-style, his shirt landing halfway into the living room. Taking my hand he stands me up. He undresses me, lays me down on the fur. I open my legs and stare up at him. His penis is fully erect, its taut head shining in the dark. I orgasm multiple times with him inside me and out, and Harold ejaculates on the mink. We lie together for a moment staring at the huge cake frosting swirl of the texturized ceiling before Harold returns the mink to the hall closet. I imagine how the darkened patch where he came will grow stiff. How the woman will flick her nail at it, wondering what the hell she rubbed up against.

We leave the way we entered. In the last half-hour or so the fire escape is much fainter against to the wall-to-wall carpet. Outside, the stars and the moon quickly fade into the white-gray sky. I can hear the garbage trucks rumbling out the gate of the city department of sanitation, a few blocks away. Right next to it, there is a horse stable that you wouldn't even know existed except for the sign. The walls are so high, you cannot see the horses, but I always look over anyway, hoping that one of them will appear on the sidewalk, much larger than I ever imagined, her hooves against the cement the only sound for miles.

Pornography

A little after six on a Sunday in July. 1968. It's muggy and the air is unmoving rather than still; a thing in itself, like another wall in the two small rooms. Whiffs of garbage, cat urine, and spaghetti steam compete for prominence until they are enfolded in layers of heat forming a stew. Another thing in itself.

"Women, let's take a seat and get going." Ti-Grace motions with the Mexican wine goblet, its chunky greenish-blue glass the color of the Caribbean. She exits the small kitchen for the small living room, which later becomes her bedroom.

The four of us shimmy laterally, to try and avoid bumping into each other as we queue for the shiny green canister of parmesan cheese. In the living room, Ti-Grace presides, and not just because it is her apartment. She always gives the impression of running things, despite *The Feminists* pledge to function cooperatively. She sits on top of what looks like an oversized high chair, near the barred window that faces the alleyway and a wall that just misses the neighbor's similarly imprisoned window. This is the third meeting of *The Feminists*. A splinter group from NOW.

Radical feminists, the press likes to say of us, raising their collective eyebrow and sowing fear in their readers.

"Let's hear what you've come up with," Ti-Grace says looking at me and Barbara.

"These two are brilliant," she says, cocking her head at us. Barbara and I sit to the right of Ti-Grace, in putty-colored folding chairs, leaving the two uncomfortable beanbags to the left of Ti-Grace, for Mary Lee and Janice, visitors to the group who may or may not stick around.

Some of our regulars, Sheila Cronan, Anne Koedt, couldn't make it tonight. With people who don't know me here, I feel like I have to prove myself all over again, a redundancy I resent. Sweat dribbles down my back, and the hot plates of spaghetti balance on our slick knees. Mary Lee and Janice stare deeply into the gluey mass, moving it around with their forks, as if they might find something to choke on.

"Pam and I plan to visit porn shops in Times Square to gauge how men respond when actual women stand next to them while they look at pictures of women spread eagle, mouths open," Barbara says.

"That's a really interesting idea," Mary Lee nods her head.

Barbara and I met Mary Lee and Janice at an Abortion Rights March three weeks ago. They introduced themselves as Columbia journalism students, and said they recognized us from a picture that appeared in the Voice about our demo at the Marriage License Bureau. They'd heard that we'd split from NOW, they said excitedly, and Barbara invited them to sit in on one of our meetings.

"That is good," Ti-Grace says, motioning with her empty fork. She places her plate on the floor, switching it out for the wine goblet.

"We went out last Saturday to do reconnaissance." I don't look at anyone but Ti-Grace.

My mother has always told people that I'm shy, perhaps to explain why I'm not pretty. Her explanation and my "shyness" are more like shame. I have not, nor have I ever been, pretty.

Mary Lee and Janice are both very pretty. I've tried to train myself not to notice or think about how women look. But beauty is something the world appreciates and rewards. These women are nice to look at. It's as if intrinsic to their beauty is certain favor, for and toward them.

Janice has begun to cut up her spaghetti into small, neat bites. Mary Lee gave up pushing the food around. Her fork rests on the side of her full plate.

"It's a perfect idea, when you think about it. Having men confront the real and the fantasy at once."

She leans forward as she speaks. Her dinner plate is perilously close to sliding from her lap and onto the dirty wood floor.

"We just walked around last weekend, we didn't actually go in anywhere. That'll be the hard part," Barbara says.

Mary Lee says, "Maybe we could go with you, write it up and shop it around?"

I've never before met anyone named Mary Lee. Her hair is golden brown to match her skin; she's all smooth surfaces. Janice is more angular. A tall, delicate blonde with skinny legs neatly folded underneath her.

"That would be wonderful," Ti Grace says.

It's time for more wine. My plate clatters to the floor and the women all turn to look at my abrupt movement. They readily turn back and focus on each other when I ignore them.

From the kitchen I listen to Barbara continue.

"Most of the hard core porn covers are of women's asses, which just reinforces men's view of women as animalistic," Barbara says.

"Asking for it all the time," Ti-Grace adds.

"You're right," Janice says. "I've noticed that, too."

Standing in the dark, narrow kitchen, I pour myself another glass of wine. For a moment I concentrate on the silence of the small space. I pretend I am alone, or abandoned here along with the detritus covering the red Formica counter tops. I finish the wine in my glass and pour another. Back to the living room, jug in hand. I set it in the center of the floor.

"Inside the covers with women's asses at eye level, as you buy the Voice, it's images of women being beaten and raped by men and dogs and bottles. The more violent the better," I say. I sit down with a thud.

Mary Lee nods, a grim, abbreviated tilt of her small chin.

Janice unfurls her long legs, a praying mantis of a woman.

"Porno is like an instruction manual," says Ti-Grace.

Another slug of wine while eyeing the gallon bottle. I try to estimate how much is left, and look at each woman's glass to gauge how fast I should drink my third glass of wine so I can get to the bottle before it is empty.

"Even the mainstream stuff," Barbara shakes her head. "I really think most people would be surprised at the level of violence depicted. It's not about fantasy if the pornography and the news reflect each other."

Quickly, a ray of sun beams through the small window. The bars are clearly delineated on the dusty wood floors, bits of dust stream into the light, dance there in the heat.

I say, "I'm working with some students at St. John's on trying to write legislation requiring mandatory brown covers for pornography on newsstands. This would limit the public availability of the images, but isn't asking for a ban. So we think we have a good chance. One of my old professors has agreed to help us out as much as she can."

Mary Lee rearranges herself on the bean bag. Little farting noises glide into the air from the deep plastic folds of the plastic cover. She struggles to sit up straight, and places her untouched spaghetti on the floor.

Ti-Grace addresses Mary Lee and Janice: "The direct actions— and I think the visits to the porn shops will get a lot of attention— they're ways to get people talking, but what we really want are laws on the books. When were you planning to start the visits to the shops, anyway?" Ti-Grace asks Barbara.

"We were thinking next weekend," Barbara says.

"Sure," I nod, draining my glass.

The sun retreats as quickly as it entered the room only moments ago, leaving the air a diffuse gray color.

Butters, Ti-Grace's orange cat, jumps up on the window sill. He snakes around the bars, and considers us for a few seconds.

The room is quiet, save the cat's trilling. Ti-Grace gets up to raise the window screen and let him in. We follow her with our eyes, and then Butters. Without acknowledging us any further, he disappears into the kitchen.

"A male has entered the house," Ti-Grace says smiling. "But he has been neutered."

Laughter is heard.

I lean back, glance at the huge ameba-shaped spill on the ceiling, like someone knocked over a huge cup of coffee.

Next to me, Janice looks down into her empty wine glass. Her gaze remains fixed on the burgundy stain that looks as if it has bled into the stem.

"There's a long piece Mary Lee and I have pitched to the Columbia Journal of Politics and Society, about how male violence impacts women's lives."

Janice looks at each of us. The room is quiet, our faces shiny with heat.

"We want to write about women's experiences with rape, and how the threat of rape and other sorts of physical violence at men's hands influences women's lives. You know, I feel like I've gone to enough Women's Groups by now to know that most women have a story or stories about being raped or almost raped."

Janice pauses. She shakes her head. "And most of them have never talked about what happened to them, before finding themselves surrounded by other women who say that happened to me, too."

Mary Lee nods. "You finally meet people who give a damn about what happened to you. The women we've spoken to who've

told people or who've tried to press charges—it didn't matter—
the men were never arrested never mind prosecuted. The police
and prosecutors spend a lot of time trying to convince women the
charges won't stick. There's the whole "what were you wearing,
had you been drinking, do you sleep around? Basically, they bully
women into thinking no one will believe them."

The mundane sound of the fan occupies the silence.

I say. "And it works. A big part of the problem is that the
judges, lawyers, and police are all fucking men. They relate to the
rapists, not to the girls. They don't want the charges to stand. We
need more women in the courts and working as police."

Ti-Grace's hands gracefully move through the air, as if she
is gathering invisible strands together, "What if we solicited a
number of pieces from different women about their rapes, and
included it in the pornography piece we're doing?"

She pauses, warming to the subject.

"It would mirror what's we're trying to do in the shops—here's
the violent depiction of a rape in a pornographic magazine—this
is the consequence in reality."

Barbara leans forward, "We could work together looking at
the how the different aspects are all related—pornography, rape,
being dismissed by the police and the courts—how the courts'
refusal to acknowledge male violence essentially gives license
to men to beat and rape women. Also, we want to talk about
what the movement is doing to end violence in women's lives.
Pam could cover the legal aspect," she says, looking at me. "The
brown cover requirement for street vendors, the rape shield laws
people are working on…it's all huge, when you think about it."

Mary Lee nods, "It's the right time. But what bothers me is that some guys are going to get off on reading about women getting raped."

She's right. It's always tempting to pretend it's just us women. But of course everything we do and say is about men, their hatred and control of us. Our hatred of them. Separatists have the right idea, being free of them altogether.

Ti-Grace shakes her head. I watch the long, ash blond strands of her hair prettily separating on her tanned shoulder. The first thing out of my mother's mouth after she met her was how she thought she was better than everyone else because she was good-looking. It was something easy for her to point to, when she doesn't trust *anyone*. My mother's unwieldy mind exercises the utmost control in her own small world: the world of me and my father. Everyone she cannot reign over, she destroys in her own mind.

"But that can't be what informs our decision," Ti-Grace continues. There are silenced women who've been raped out there, who need to hear these accounts. There are other people who've never even thought about rape, or what it means personally, politically. Giving voice to women's stories has to be more important."

Like Artaud. *Signaling through the flames.*

"I agree," Janice says.

Mary Lee frowns. Quietly, she says, "Yeah, I know. I just hate to think of anyone getting off on it."

I nod. "And there are things people don't even think about, like the physical pain, being torn apart like that when you're not receptive. We need people to really think about what rape is. They think it's titillating, but it's a physical and emotional assault meant to inflict pain and to control women. We need to change the conversation about rape."

Ti-Grace says, "Let's get women writing."

I STAND, GRAB THE WINE and pour everyone a last glass. I swallow its soft glow, the light spangling on the liquid surface. Everyone relaxes and begins to talk, first about who to solicit writing from, followed by the seemingly universal, mundane talk of the week ahead, meaning work. The others all have jobs, whereas, I haven't worked in over two years. When these conversations start, I am acutely aware of how work is another aspect of life that makes people acceptable to each another. Like being pretty, having a boyfriend or a girlfriend, a home, children. After I got my law degree from St. John's, I was offered an interview for a clerkship with the Supreme Court of Atlanta. My mother waved the offer letter in front of my face like an accusation.

"You can't do for yourself," she spat. "You'd be dead without your father and me!"

My mother's hot breathe was so near, along with the sound of the letter slapping against the air with certainty. My eyes snapped closed just before I watched my father walk from the room.

He'd been so pleased for me when I told him about the interview, and I'd told him first.

I wander into the kitchen with the empty wine bottle. The voices and laughter of Ti-Grace, Barbara, Janice and Mary Lee recede.

I once overheard my mother say: "She would've drowned the girls, like kittens, if she could've gotten away with it." Nine girls to the four boys, my aunts and uncles. My grandmother's sons and my mother's brothers, the boys like hope manifest, good omens to the girls' dead ends. I always wondered why my mother wouldn't have wanted to be different from her own. But that's not how it works, generally. Also, I envied her miserable child self. She had her sisters, people around. I was alone with my father only, who slipped away, around corners and into the basement, while she raged against me. I always stayed perfectly still and silent. At five, I thought I knew the playing dead rules. But there were no rules.

"Pammy?" Barbara asks, turning the overhead light on.

Barbara and I met four years ago, as roommates, both just graduated from New York University. For a while our Prince Street apartment became a hub of women, meetings and protest posters, spaghetti dinners just like this one, almost every night. Together we read Colette and Anais Nin as if we were the only two people in the world who knew of them, our discovery a blessed secret.

I follow Barbara's glance to where the roaches scurry through the counter seams. It is impossible to discern where they've gone, exactly.

"I was just thinking about that time we stayed out all night, driving around to all those colleges," I say.

Barbara and I had heard about a group that were painting chalk outlines of rape victims where rapes had occurred at local colleges. The colleges didn't want the rapes publicized. I can't even remember how we ended up finding out about the group. We never knew their names or saw them again.

"That was an amazing feeling," Barbara smiles.

The painted outlines made the front page of the Times, along with quotes from three college presidents about the cost of the property damage. They had no choice but to disclose the rapes.

"Good thing we weren't caught." She leans against the counter.

"I couldn't have sat for the bar," I say, as if it mattered that I had at this point. It's already been three years since I finished law school and passed the bar exam. I was drunk. I don't remember any of it, law school or the exam.

"How are you?" Barbara asks in that tone that tries to be easy and yet telegraphs that she knows, along with many others, how I am. A lump forms in my throat. I turn and toss the wine bottle in the garbage.

"I'm good," I say. There's nothing to tell, like with other people. Barbara for instance. She continues, "I'm going to Kenya in January to conduct my captive chimp study with wild chimpanzees."

I smile and say that's wonderful, and I mean it.

Barbara is at Columbia now. A Ph. D candidate in the Women's Studies Department, with an office and a research grant.

I told Dr. Tucec that the year I lived with Barbara was the only year in my life that I've ever felt like what I thought other people must feel like.

"And what do you mean by what other people must feel like?" he asked.

"Like a human being," I replied, angrily. "Someone who wakes up and does things during the day, like their lives are normal. I don't feel like I'm in my life, "I said. "That year, I did, though."

"So do you think the best of your life is over? You have your whole life in front of you, Pam," he'd said, leaning forward so that I heard the soft leather of his chair gather.

I laughed at him and he tried to look composed. People have these things they say, all of them, the exact same things. Even psychiatrists, who you would think would know better.

"It's not something I think," I said. "It's something I know."

What I thought at that moment was how tempting it is to believe that plays don't reflect real moments in life, moments when you realize something essential about yourself. A failure of courage, exposed. Just like in a play, my failure was no secret. It had an audience, however small. I saw it the eyes of my brother and sister, and Barbara, and some of my aunts and uncles, when I told them I wasn't going to the interview in Atlanta.

I wasn't going anywhere. That everyone knew or had to be told, my mother liked that. She'd won.

"And at some point, it was too late, you've said before? Barbara thought you were moving to Atlanta, and she moved?" Dr. Tucec prodded, making a steeple with his fingers.

I shrugged.

"Everyone I knew moved for teaching jobs or to go back to school," I said. "Most of the people I knew then are gone."

"But you're still close to Barbara. You still have some of those friends from that time, and your work in the Women's Movement. Why is it different?" The leather shifted under his weight, sounding oddly like plastic. I looked up

"I don't know, it just is. I feel like a mind without a body. I don't know how to do things, or want to. Every day. All day. Waking and bathing, dressing and working and eating. I just can't want to do it all."

This was all in the beginning, when Dr. Tucec and I still talked on occasion.

The last time I was admitted to St. Vincent's one of the nurses said, "I'm surprised you're not dead with all the meds that witch doctor has you on."

Dr. Tucec, like every psychiatrist I've ever met, was trained to believe in the triumph of pills over people like me. There's always the little get to know you dance in the beginning, for show. A couple of slots for the fifty minute hour before the demotion to maintenance visits of fifteen minutes. After the initial interviews, their eyes wander to the prescription pad before your fifteen minutes are even up.

Behind Barbara, Janice and Mary Lee, plates in hand, shimmy into the kitchen. Janice fills the sink with hot water and I listen to the dinner plates rocket to the bottom of the basin. Steam clouds the air. In the other room, Ti-Grace talks to the cat, asking him where he has been all day.

There are whole years of my life I don't remember. The year I lived with Barbara I remember, but I'd rather not. That's what I said to Dr. Tucec. It's like it was a mistake. A time when I thought not only could I change my life, but the lives of all women. It was my certainty that is painful to remember.

I can feel the three women behind me, looking at each other as I drift from the kitchen, my mind an exposed underside, rumpled and soft and livid; something awakened to its essential self. My plain face red and crying, made ugly.

The cat thumps to the floor as Ti-Grace stands and walks toward me.

I raise my hand to shield myself and to stop Ti-Grace from trying to reach me. As the door closes, I hear the voices of Barbara and Mary Lee: "Did Pam leave?" and 'What happened?"

Out on the street no one looks at me, or if they do, it's to look above or to the side of me, to step around me as if I don't exist. A relief, a reprieve. I watch myself walk away, head down, hands in my pockets, growing smaller and smaller as I pass fruit and flower and newspaper stands, everyone in their place. Antonin Artaud wrote that he didn't wish to die, but to never have been born. This idea excited me so much when I was younger that you would have thought it was an option: that I could be sucked off the planet, until even the empty space left behind faded, disappeared. Not an option, but the idea of it still has had an aspirational quality for me, and has since I was about five years old, and knew nothing of Artaud or the vocabulary of existentialism. I knew only of my mother and father, of our being yoked together, randomly. And forever. I was *theirs* and I wanted out.

"I'm not depressed," I once told Dr. Tucec. "I'm demoralized. There's a difference."

He didn't agree, said my intellectualizing was a defense.

"Some defense!" I laughed.

I watch myself enter my building. The tarnished brass door handle and trim still manage to glint under the street light. The

sound of the heavy wooden door echoes in the marble hallways,
underscoring the finality of its closing, and locking me in.

Set on Fire

A TAMBOURINE CLATTERS INSIDE MY head. People chant, some parade skips down Thompson Street to Washington Square Park. Saturday mornings are full of marches and face painting and flutes and drums and tambourines. I turn on the floor, crack my eye, like a wound, opening. The pain resides not just in my eyes and head, but to the tissue and the bone.

I have a talent for seeing through the pinpoint of men's eyes to where all they want to do is beat a woman to death, or near to death.

The boy last night was a boy. Under eighteen maybe. A young freshman. Silently, he followed me back to my apartment and locked the door after us. When I put the light out, he turned it back on. Without speaking he pointed. I removed my blouse, bra, pants, and shoes. His belt slithered though the loops of his trousers. He took a flask out of his jacket, opened it, and handed it to me. I took a pull on Scotch so smooth I finished what was left. Three fingers, four. I felt like I'd been set on fire. A light went out in my head.

When I next woke, it was the middle of the night. My breasts and ass had puffy, fluid welts that made it hard for me to move. I started to scream and crawl for cover, trying to scramble under the bed, but I couldn't fit. My landlord came in. He said that I was a disgusting whore. He said he would call my father if I didn't shut up. A light went out in my head for the second time.

I inch over to the bedside table on my stomach, my chest raised so I don't make contact with the floor. At the bottom of a deep drawer I fish around for the bottle of vodka and my medications: Parnate and Valium and Dexedrine. I push myself up, balancing on my left hip, and shake the pills into my outstretched palm. The bright yellow and orange dyes seem to dissolve in the vodka, leaving a chalky, bitter taste on my tongue that I like. It tastes like I'm doing something. Feeling something. Or about to feel nothing. I lie down on my left side and wait to go numb.

David Frost Shows His Large Teeth

SOME GUY WHO WORKS ON the David Frost show called me at four in the afternoon yesterday. I don't even know how they got my phone number, unless it was through the Voice reporter. A guest had canceled due to illness, he said, and then asked if I could make it tomorrow afternoon. "David is interested in your essay "Man-Hating," he continued.

I said 'No, no,' and then cupped my hand over the receiver when my friend Kathrine, a new friend of mine from the last time I was hospitalized at St. Vincent's, asked who it was. She grabbed the phone and said, "Yes, she'll be there with bells on, man. Give us the information."

Though they didn't say who canceled, we looked it up in the TV Guide. It was Tiny Tim.

BEHIND THE CURTAIN, THE STUDIO looks like a dank garage. A pewter-colored light predominates, with mechanical things parked all over the place. The young man who fetched me from the Green Room stands behind me, his breath on the back of my neck. About twenty minutes ago, while I was still in the safety of the Green Room, Kathrine gave me four Dexedrine. "For stage fright," she said with her sweet smile, placing them in the center of my palm as a nurse might. "Down the hatch, Pammy," she said, pouring me a second glass of the wine that is available for guests. My heart itself feels open and calm in my chest. Floating there. I smile.

David Frost begins to introduce me. "Man-Hating is the title of Pamela Kearon's provocative and troubling essay. Ms. Kearon is here with us tonight."

They man behind me whispers, "Go, go, go." I step from the dank behind-the-scenes air, to the tangerine and lavender colored set. Two bright orange chairs face each other, with microphones that twist from their armrests. Warm lights hang from the rafters, and succeed in obscuring the first couple of rows of the audience. The successive rows are a happy blur to me. They clap, a very nice sound, I decide. I wait for a moment, smiling. David Frost stands, and motions for me to sit. He's so close, I can see the large pores in his beakish nose. I smell his aftershave.

He crosses his legs and turns toward me. "Tell us the premise of your essay."

His British accent and the sound of his voice disarms me, it's so familiar. I remember his interview with the Beatles, with John Lennon, with other revolutionaries, Leroi Jones and Julian Bond. I smile again. It's so fucking weird to be with David Frost.

I cross my legs like him. I fumble in my pocket and find a cigarette. A young woman from behind the curtain runs out with a small table and an ashtray. She places it of my left, so quickly that all I see is the flash of her red top, a lock of blond hair.

"The premise is a simple one: that women hating men is not an aberrant or unexpected response, but rather natural response to being controlled, and to being viewed a less than human by an oppressor. Afro-American slaves hated their owners; women hate theirs."

The audience claps and David Frost nods his head. I light my cigarette, pinch it between my fingers for a quick drag, the nicotine a peculiar kind of food. When the clapping subsides, David Frost looks like he's about to add something, but I'm antsy. I can feel the audience waiting, ready to listen to me. I turn slightly, look out at the black-gray mass lacking individual faces, all the way to the horizon of the back row. It's exciting, how far away the back row is. How I am talking to them.

"The common perception is that man hating is solely a radical feminist practice. In my essay, I maintain that is neither radical nor particularly feminist. It's a human response to having your autonomy restricted, and in some cases, destroyed."

"That's very interesting. I'm not sure hatred is the most productive response, but I see what you're getting at," he says.

Still directing my eyes to the audience I say, "No one wants an oppressed class to be angry, so anger is maligned, seen as useless, as you say. People talk of angry black men—who are so frightening to the mainstream because we know how brutalized the Afro-American race has been in our culture—enslaved, beaten, lynched. We know that they hate us, that that is only natural given their treatment at our hands. People's fear of blacks' anger, or women's anger—it proves the point of my essay."

"Yes, but what is the point of anger? Where does it get you?" David Frost's voice rises an octave, alarmed, questioning.

"Anger is an active and creative force. To view it simply as destructive trivializes its inherent power," I say. "It's an expression of a truth that the oppressor must acknowledge. The expression and the acknowledgement are necessary for transformation to occur, ultimately. For us to move from a highly stratified society where powerful white men rule everyone else—send poor white and Afro-American men to war, legislate and rape women's bodies, and block access to opportunity to everyone but people who look and think like them—to a color, gender, and class blind society where we really do have equal opportunity for all."

More clapping. Not thunderous; a smattering, along with a woman hollering. I laugh when I recognize the voice of Katherine. "Sisters of the World, Unite!" She walks toward me and David Frost from behind the curtain, no doubt having escaped the Green Room without anyone realizing it. David Frost follows my gaze and notices her just before the guy from backstage grabs her. He turns to face me, as if a woman hadn't been making a beeline toward us. He steeples his fingers and leans forward.

"It's an ambitious agenda, I'll grant you that. I just don't know that I agree that the way to this egalitarian society is through anger, and, of course, sometimes, increasingly, violence."

"There's no choice," I shrug. "Those in power fight to keep that power. Peaceful revolutions are wishful thinking. They don't exist."

David Frost laughs, showing his large teeth.

He fears me, but not just me. His smile is a lie to himself that

I am not the 'what if' of all these angry groups coming to fuck everything up.

"We'll have to end on that somber note," he says, extending his arms, then clasping his hands together. Leaning over he thanks me. The guy from before walks toward us, his clipboard tight against his chest. As I rise to meet him, I realize David Frost is gone. The spotlights click off and a more diffuse, bland light dims the colorful set. The low murmur of the audience headed toward the exits sounds most like the official end of the show, more than the lights going off and David Frost leaving the stage. The back row emptying. I'm still high but not high enough to not feel a twinge of the end of something that passed by, as if I were staring through a train window, in a blur. The blur is good and bad. It makes me feel like I'm leaving a place I've never been, but I couldn't do any of it otherwise. If not for the booze and Katherine's large pills, the same orange color of David Frost's set, there would have been no David Frost. The Voice writer was more insightful than he knew, christening my 'inebriated eloquence,' the symbiosis of drugs and booze and me, forging a whole other person who remembers nothing and therefore can do and say anything.

I hear the guy talking next to my ear. "We've made dinner reservations for you and your friend at Sardis, compliments of the show. There's a taxi waiting downstairs." He puts his arm around my shoulders without actually touching me, herding me off the set. I'm not hungry. I will never be hungry again.

Once I'm backstage, Katherine rushes toward me from the Green Room. She sometimes thinks she is Van Gogh, and has been arrested, several times, for trying to remove her (or his) paintings from MOMA. Also, she's a nudist. She has been arrested for that, too. Naked on trains and buses and sidewalk cafes. She's been on a good run, lately. Florid still, but not gaining the notice of law enforcement, who feel and rub against her body, as they throw her into the back of their cars. They've probably done much worse. Her life is also a blur.

"Dinner's on them, Pammy!" she screams at me, her long brown hair, its bangs, shaping her face. She smiles so genuinely she must look like the girl she once was, before the illness. Before the psych wards and the arrests, from Indiana, where she's from, to Miami and New York, cities she landed in without memory of how or why. I look at my other friends, from school and the movement, and I think: "You know nothing." I feel now that I have to be close only to people who know how it is not to trust yourself to be yourself, but Van Gogh, fear, despair, a glass of vodka. Crucified Jesus. Anything. You could be anything, most of it bad. Only very occasionally are you good. Uppers are the good. Nudge me to the surface of the water, where I see the sights, and take a breath, before the inevitable drowning.

Katherine grabs my hand and pulls me back though the dark corridor to the Green Room, laughing all the way. We quickly finish off the wine, handing the bottle back and forth between us. Watching us, his face smooth and blank, the guy says the taxi is waiting. Katherine says, "It's the hall monitor." Once we begin to laugh we can't stop. Wine dribbles out my nose and from between my lips. Katherine shrieks that she has to pee, walking funny, then tearing into the small adjoining bathroom, both of us hysterical. The guy leans against the door jam, and I grab my coat from the back of a chair for something to do now the wine is caput. "Made it!" Katherine says, the toilet still gurgling behind her. For the first time I notice some expression on the guy's face. It softens a little, like he might like us now that we're leaving. Or because we're leaving. He hustles us down a narrow staircase I don't remember from the way in. He thanks me for coming with his hand on the door, opening it for us in one seamless motion as we are swept away. The taxi driver holds another door and we duck into the back seat. Outside, car horns honk and the blue and red neon lights bleed together. The shiny leather seats are cracked and worn, our heads thrown back in laughter, and with the force of acceleration.

"Everything is purple," I say to no one.

In the Palm of God's Hand

IT IS CHRISTMAS EVE, 1977. I'm on a cot in my parents' attic, pissing myself and crying. I tell my niece Mia about the men. The NYU boys. How I like to be beaten. Ask for it. Even through several layers of delirium, I feel her recoil at my words, my face screwed up like a weeping fist. At fourteen, she has enough of a sense of what is socially acceptable to find me disgusting. No longer am I her cool aunt who lives in Greenwich Village and smokes weed. I am much more. Like a character from the Flannery O'Connor story collection I gave her for her birthday last year, I am grotesque, far easier to read about than to experience.

On the occasion of my confession, her family is visiting from upstate. Earlier today, my brother Charlie, Mia's father, picked me up from St. Vincent's. Home from the mental institution for the holidays. We said hardly anything the whole ride from Manhattan to Canarsie. I got out of the car during gridlock and squatted in the bushes along the highway to pee. I had to pee. I left the passenger-side door open, and when I got back in the car Charlie wouldn't look at me. He said I could get arrested for that. This came out quietly and not with recrimination. Just a statement. He didn't know what else to say.

Charlie walked into the house ahead of me. I dumped my bag on the floor and said that I was going upstairs to lie down. My father said you're staying in the attic since Mia is sleeping in your old room. He was bent over the table, setting it. My mother was in the kitchen, smoking, her lips barely opened and her eyes blank with aggression. She ordered my father not to wait on me. "You have enough to do," she said.

Dr. Tucec knows about the boys. Him, and now Mia. Incredulously, Mia asks, "How? Why would they?" She is just a baby. She can't fathom the logistics, physical, emotional, of meeting men in the park in broad daylight, or worse yet, at night. Men, who without a word, answer the pleading in my eyes.

She doesn't ask why about me. Either she has known about me all along, or she has been told by her parents that I am a sick person.

"Grandma hated me," I cry. "She said I was ugly. She said she wished I were never born."

"What about Grandpa?" Mia asks. "Why didn't he help you?"

I can hear the theme music for the movie of the week, *Columbo*. Also, company. Family entering the house with coffee cakes, bundled up against the cold. My mother will tell them I have the flu.

"He was scared of her. He is still. They all are," I say.

"I should go down and say hi," Mia says. "I'll come back later."

THE TV WAS TURNED DOWN when the family arrived, but not all the way off. I can still hear its voices, distinct from the real voices, which are louder and less precise. The family brave enough to visit still are probably Uncle George and Aunt Mary, Katherine and John. Charlie and his wife Eileen and my father will be happy to see them. My mother will give them nothing. Earlier, she will have told Charlie and Eileen and my father not to encourage them to stay. "Don't bring out the cold cuts." The family is used to it. They came to see Charlie and his wife and Mia, not my mother. They will ask him to stop by before they leave, and Charlie will feel relieved that he will get to see everyone under normal circumstances.

I'M SINKING FARTHER AND FARTHER into the cot, rotting there. My nightgown is wet with perspiration and urine, the cot soaked through. A weight seeps into the bottom of my throat and falls into my gut, a pain as familiar as it is leaden. I turn to try and find a position where it doesn't hurt. I'm so cold. Finally, I stop moving. The pain doesn't recede so much as settle.

The built-in drawers in the attic are a reddish brown wood, heavily shellacked. They hold funeral cards with the Virgin Mary or St. Christopher on the front, ordered for my mother's many dead brothers by her sisters. The sisters, the aunts, are all still alive. There is a small space in the drawers for my father's WWII medals. And always one or two of those huge balls with rubber bands, crossing and crisscrossing, so tightly wound I always imagine the sound of the bands snapping whenever I come across them. The small, sloped attic roof has patterned green wallpaper that looks like cities and then faces, looming over me.

After the company leaves, Eileen, my brother's wife, comes up. She holds me under my elbow and rests me against the wall while she removes the peed-on sheets, then my nightgown. She pats me down with a washcloth, pulls a clean gown over my head, and tucks the excess sheets under the thin mattress.

I don't know if she has been instructed to help by my father or her husband. Or if it was her idea. If no one said anything to her but Mia.

I cry and break into sobs. Eileen says, "It's okay Pam."

I listen to her and my brother at the bottom of the stairs:

"How could they let her out in this condition? What are we supposed to do with her?"

"I don't know," says my brother. "I called Dr. Tucec, but he hasn't gotten back to me."

Mia comes up with toast and tea.

"Can you try to eat a little?" she asks. She pulls over a chair. I gulp the hot tea to try and wash the lump of flour down my throat. I gag and spit it out, burning the inside of my mouth and dribbling tobacco-colored tea down the front of the clean nightgown.

Mia places the plate and cup on a dresser drawer. She looks out the third-floor window, opaque with frost etchings, a primitive accounting scratched onto the glass. She reaches a fingernail to the pane and scrapes.

"I've told my parents I need to speak to them about this," she says. "We're going to see George and Mary tomorrow night after dinner. I'll do it then."

I can tell she is certain that her words will help for being spoken.

"I wrote to your father once," I say. "When he was in Dunoon. I asked him to help me. He didn't."

"He must not have gotten it," she offers.

"You don't understand," I cry. "Carol and Charlie left. They got out."

I don't say that I didn't. The heaviness and pain in my throat and chest is replaced by hopelessness.

"Leave me alone." I've talked enough. I am tired.

Being on my side, Mia didn't expect this. The air around her small person perceptibly changes. She feels like she's been hit. Her eyes burn. She hovers cot-side, thinking she might touch me. Eventually, after her breathing has gotten too loud for her to stand, she gathers my plate and teacup and she leaves.

It has gotten dark. Light from the streetlamp slants down the greenish wallpaper.

I hear goodbyes and Merry Christmases from the family I haven't seen in years. My mother won't get up from her chair or say goodbye.

When I was little, I used to spend Saturdays and Sundays in the attic. Sometimes I hid in the long narrow closet where the tweed jackets that my father no longer wore hung together in the dark. I ran my hands over their filled-out shoulders before I crouched below them, wondering when and where he used to wear them. I'd never known him to go out. Or her. Their lives and mine were contained in the number of small rooms where my mother made her life, and ours.

Despite being on the top floor, to me the attic has always had the feeling of being submerged, watery and sunken. I float on the ocean floor. My body is so light. It rests in the palm of God's hand, as the red and green and blue shadows from the neighbors' Christmas lights stagger across the wall.

Their Eyes Filled With Warmth That Is Neither Warranted Nor Returned

WE PASS FROM THE DAMP cold of the subway to the biting cold of the subway platform, Letty, Harold, and I. Canarsie is deserted. The light snow that has fallen all afternoon has stopped but whirls around. Icy pin pricks assault our faces and the traffic lights manically swing. It is twelve, thirteen degrees. My toes have gone numb, but are past the stinging pain of a few moments ago, on the train. The vodka, Valium, and the hit of blotter insulate me from the worst of it.

I grope around in my satchel to make sure Mia's present didn't fall out somewhere. The three of us spent over an hour trying to figure out how to assemble it this morning. Harold ran drills to make sure it worked, and managed to concoct an impressive finale for its brief flight. I finger its outline, and reposition it against my wallet for safekeeping.

"Where we headed, Pammy?" Harold yells back to me.

"Go about five blocks, 'til you hit 92nd Street. Then right," I say, motioning my hand through the air, at the back of Harold's head.

I turn to look back at Letty. Two dogs appear from the squalling snow. They straggle behind her. The one in front, a female, I assume, follows us longingly. The male follows her, sometimes trying to mount her when she stays still long enough, which isn't that often. Letty wears what looks like a pelt, a combed suede jacket with fur trim around the neck, the sleeves, and the hem. Maybe the coat attracted the dogs? I keep looking over my shoulder at them. Neither Letty nor Harold seems to have noticed them.

"Look behind you," I yell to Letty. "You have an entourage."

Letty looks at me like she sees nothing. She runs her hand through the blowing snow like it is a fine lace.

A blinking plow rushes past us, not plowing but barreling down Canarsie Ave. It's Christmas Eve. We're going to my parents for dinner. It's dark out but I don't know the time. We may have missed dinner but there's always leftovers. My brother Charlie is visiting so he'll have gone to the commissary already. There will be plenty of booze.

Out of nowhere, like she's known all along the dog was following her but didn't want to look at it, Letty turns around and says, "Go home," her hand raised in command.

The dog approaches familiarly, like she knows Letty. She is the sweetest being on the earth I see from her warm smile. "I love this dog," I say. "Look at her accepting us without question. Trusting us. Your coat."

Harold says nothing. He knows nothing. He's up ahead with his hands in his pockets. He wears a parka with orange tape on the elbows and one of the pockets. He found it on a bus a couple of weeks ago.

"My father loves dogs," I say, thinking of Blacky, dead for ten years already.

"Yeah?" Letty asks, crying now. I can hear it in her voice and I walk back to her.

"I'm so cold, aren't you cold?" she asks. She stops and the female dog licks her hand. The male hangs back, considering her and me.

Looking at the dog for the first time, Letty again directs, "Go home! Go!"

The female backs up, toward the other dog. Letty issues another desperate command, "Go home. GO HOME, GO HOME!"

The dogs run off, the female now glancing over her shoulder at me.

"We shouldn't have let them follow us." This she says quietly. I'm standing so close to her I feel her breathing beside me.

"Now they might get lost," she says helplessly. Her long, thin hair whips around her face. Bubbles form at the sides of her mouth and her nose runs. "What a shit night," she says.

I think of the Little Match Girl in her doorway. Of the skinny dogs, still hopeful that there is someone they can follow inside.

Harold realizes we're not right behind him when he reaches the corner of 92nd Street and Canarsie Ave. He stops there, tipping his head back to watch the snow falling sideways through the glow of the streetlight. He looks warm in his stolen coat, comfortable. My movement is restricted by my soaked wool coat, heavy like armor.

I stop next to Harold. When Letty reaches us, I take her by the elbow to guide her to the right. I nod down Canarsie Ave., toward the lit-up Santa and reindeer displays, weaving in and out of the Jesus and Mary and the manger scenes. Red and blue and green lights twist around the fences that close off each 8-by-10 front yard, many of them concrete slabs with tufts of grass sprouting from their cement seams.

"We only have about a half a block," I tell Letty.

Harold starts to sing, "Here we go a' caroling upon a Christmas Eve, ba ba ba de da de da . . ."

Letty has a stoic look on her face. Harold gives her a friendly bump in the shoulder and smiles down at her, "A monkey on my sleeve," he rhymes."

"Look, Nazareth," he says, pointing at the Gannon's' yard. They have a life-size Jesus and Mary in a stable. He swoops Letty into his arms and rushes over, one of his legs skidding from below him. He rights himself before spilling the two of them on the sidewalk. Harold is graceful. It's what makes him such a good thief; he is lithe and surefooted. Unlocking the Gannon's' gate he evicts baby Jesus from his crèche and lowers Letty's ass into a dish basin filled with straw. The basin flips from beneath her and she lies at Mary's feet, laughter racking her shoulders. Together, Harold and I yank her up. Surprisingly, the Gannon's' home remains perfectly dark and still.

A couple of doors away, except for the silvery hue in the living room that means the TV is on, there are no lights on at my house either. There are no decorations in our yard, but you can see the outline of the unlit tree against the sheers. The front gate creaks when I unlatch it, opens out when it would more logically open in. A light suddenly appears from my parents' bedroom window.

"Come on," I say, leading the way up the front steps and onto the small screened-in porch that no one ever uses.

"Dad, dad, open up. It's me." I pound on the front door and wait, stomping the snow and cold from my feet. I hear the chain sliding, and the locks click open. I see my father peering out at us.

"Pammy," he says, opening the door. "Come in and I'll get you some food."

My father is stooped these days, not from age but from something else that I attribute to living with my mother, his ability to stand upright leached from his bones.

If he notices Harold and Letty, he doesn't acknowledge them. We follow him into the kitchen and he begins retrieving leftovers from the oven. I hear my mother coming down the stairs. She is only five foot tall and shrinking. I look at her deeply bowed legs and the natty housedress she wears day and night. It's threadbare and the cheap snaps are rusted. I ignore her.

No one would know, looking at her, that she is the kind of person who pushed her child down the stairs because it felt good to do it, like filling her lungs with air for a deafening scream. Or most people don't know. Over the years, I've noticed Eileen, Charlie's wife, catch on. Not that my mother would ever hurt Mia. It's Eileen she desires to push and to hurt. There have been visits where mother won't talk to or look at Eileen. During other visits, it's like those cruel, interminable days never passed between them like freezing air in which it was difficult to move.

Letty and Harold say "hello" and introduce themselves to my mother.

"What did you do today," she asks, looking at Harold. She reaches over to turn on a black and white television the size of a book cover. The manic sensibility of *I Love Lucy* enters the fray.

Harold says, "I worked for a few hours."

"We watched him, from a coffee shop across the street," Letty adds.

"He's a beggar." I say this before my mother can ask him what he does. "He went to Macy's and stood next to the Salvation Army Santa."

"That's work, too," my mother says companionably.

Harold laughs. "That's what I say."

My mother is solicitous toward my friends. On the rare occasions when she and I are alone these days, she says things like, "I know things have been hard for you, Pammy, because you are so smart. And shy. It's a disease, do you know that? I read that once." She has recast herself and me in some other story.

No one says anything to my father, and I can't remember if he ever met them or not. He may have but he doesn't let on either way. He shuffles and stoops, placing food on the Formica table, turkey, mashed potatoes, canned peas, and yams. They are lukewarm and withered from the oven. My mother sits next to me and lights a cigarette. I get up and go into the dining room. I was right. My brother went to the base and got my father enough booze to last for three months, until he visits again.

"Get us some glasses, Dad," I say.

I pour, filling three tumblers with Smirnoff. "Do you want one?" I ask my dad.

He looks at my mother and shakes his head. She doesn't drink. But she likes that my father does, or at least when she has sanctioned it. It gives her something else to deride him for. But tonight, it's too late. He's already had his drink. She raises her fingers to her mouth to inhale the cigarette she just lit, somehow suggesting she might take a swipe at him if he has another.

GREEDILY, LETTY GULPS HER DRINK. Harold lights a cigarette. He leans back in the chair and releases a thin stream of smoke.

"You can go to bed," I say, not looking at either of my parents. "When we finish eating, we can sleep down here."

No one is hungry. The food arrayed at the table's center is lackluster, dry and congealed.

I take a swig of the vodka; it trickles down my throat and covers the ragged hole in my chest.

My father looks into space, another thing he does a lot of. My mother says, "Turn off the lights when you're done. Come on Howard."

Letty laughs into her coat sleeve.

Harold blows smoke rings. He hasn't touched his drink yet.

I am so tired suddenly, my limbs dead weight now that I can feel them.

"I gotta lie down," I say.

I throw myself on the couch in the living room. My father has followed me.

"Do you need a blanket?"

"Leave me alone." I turn on my side. "Go away."

Glass breaks in the kitchen and he goes away. "Wow," I hear

Letty say, and "I'm sorry." She is laughing.

My mother says, "Get that."

She won't have looked at my father but will have seen him nonetheless. I know he will hurry in, bend, and sweep the noisy glass shards into one of the several dustbins around the house for his use.

A few seconds later, imperious, my mother marches through the living room, she mounts the stairs. My father follows after her.

"Remember to turn out the lights," she says.

"Yeah." I put a pillow over my head to block their figures ascending, the light from the kitchen, and the sound of Lucy from my head.

HAROLD IS SCREWING ME WHEN I wake up. We are under the dining room table. The right side of my head aches, down into my eye, a hissing cockroach, injured and living in my skull.

"Get off me," I say.

Harold moans, "Wait, wait." He orgasms so hard that I'm turned on. I imagine the narrow corridor of my dark, glistening cunt filled with Harold's cock. I grip his shoulders and we disappear into an opening in the surface of the world.

When I open my eyes, I see my father's slippers against the thin wall-to-wall carpet. Harold's breath is heavy in my ear and we are stuck together at our chests, his penis having deflated and slipped from inside me, cold and wet against my thigh. In the next second the slippers are gone, and I hear singing. I think it's singing. Letty. Wailing at the Wailing Wall, her voice giddy and carried away, then despairing. I laugh. The stairs moan under the beetlelike hunch of my father's shoulders

The sun rises. I watch it spread over the burnt orange rug. My flesh goose bumps with the cold. I crawl out from under the table. Harold snores. I climb over Letty's feet where she has passed out near the bathroom door. I pee.

Little feet pad into the bathroom. My niece, Mia, steps around Letty. I pull my pants up.

Mia points. "What's wrong with your eye?"

In the medicine cabinet mirror I see a red, swollen lump has erupted on my bottom lid. A salty crust has sealed part of it shut.

I run the tap and rinse off small granules that tear at the papery skin near my eyelashes.

"I have a sore. It's okay."

In the living room, Mia opens one end of each present under the tree of those addressed to her. She peers at whatever it is, then expertly refolds the paper, ticking off each gift in her mind. At six, already she has the capacity to be wildly disappointed in her parents' lack of knowledge of her essential character. Still, she's overjoyed about the sneaking.

Just about finished with her work, she says, "Grandma and Grandpa wouldn't let me watch you on TV the other night. They said you went on to call men pigs."

"They were right," I laugh. "Not all men," I add. "Well, it might be all of them. You know how you have mean kids at school? It's normal that you don't like them, because they're mean to you. And to other people. They're bullies, right?"

This seems obvious enough to her. She nods and says, "Yeah."

"All I did was say that men were mean to women, and that it made sense that women would not like men because of that. That it was normal, not crazy for women to feel that way."

Mia nods again. I can't tell if she really understands or if she's pretending to be grown up enough to understand. Both?

I touch her hair, the ends of it are thin, and light from the sun.

We both look up, toward the window. A car shushes by. Soon, everyone will be up and moving.

"I don't think I'm going to stay for all of this." I raise my arms at the room, sweeping across the tree and its many presents. "Is that okay?"

Mia raises her eyebrows and quickly nods, the automatic gesture conciliatory, adult.

"I wanted to see you. I always do. You know that."

I reach under the tree.

"Here, go ahead and open this one."

In one stroke, the tissue paper is devoured.

Carefully, she examines her gift, looking at each wing and the tail. She squints at the bottom and a smile breaks across her face.

She winds the screw on the undercarriage, and sends the mechanical dove toward the ceiling. It lurches into the air above the living room and just when we both think it might plummet to the floor, it soars and a twenty-dollar bill falls from its tail. Harold figured that part out, rehearsing the bird this morning to get it right.

Mia's huge brown eyes fill with wonder. She jumps into my lap and buries her head in my neck.

"Thank you Aunt Pam. I love it so much."

"You're welcome. We all had fun putting it together and making sure it worked right."

The bird falls eventually, landing on a chair seat. Mia runs to it and takes it in her hands, as if it might be wounded.

"Don't forget the twenty," I remind her, pointing toward the TV tray leg, where the tightly rolled bill has fallen.

Mia crouches down, resting her butt on her little padded feed, a tiny, amazing little animal. Perfect in all ways. She doesn't seem human yet.

"The dove will be more fun outside. Make sure you get your mom and dad to play with you later. I'm going to wake Harold and Letty and we're going to *Hit the Road, Jack.* You want to help me? Why don't you tickle Harold's toes, and I'll blow on Letty's face?"

On hands and knees, Mia begins to creep over to where Harold has stopped snoring, and is so far out he's barely breathing.

Letty farts and Mia and my eyes involuntarily widen as we look at each other. She squeals and jumps onto me, grabbing at my blouse so that it comes undone. I roll over and she tumbles off me and onto the floor. Her small enclosed feet kick as I tickle her, tapping my shoulder like pelts of rain.

I don't want to wake anyone. Or see them.

"Shhh. Help me with these two louts." I motion to Letty and Harold, sleeping the sleep of the dead.

The last time Mia and I were at my parents together was in July. I'd brought over a box of kittens that I'd found in the alley near my apartment, and she and I fed them warm milk with an eyedropper in the basement. "They look like moles," she observed as she carefully scooped one into her palm. She loves animals.

"Let's go to Africa when I grow up," she said. "That's where they have lions and tigers."

We shook on it over the silent gray mass in the shoebox, the ugly basement room transformed by the idea of the future.

"So long, little sister," Harold calls from the front sidewalk. Letty blows her a kiss, "Merry Christmas, little woman."

"I wish you could stay." Mia buries her head into my waist, holding me tight.

"I'll ask your parents if we can come get you tomorrow, take you to a movie or something. How does that sound?"

"Yes! Yes!" she exclaims, tugging on my arms.

"I'll call them later. I got to go." I pull away. "It's cold out here, you should get back inside."

"Okay," she nods.

She watches us from the window, the whole way down 92nd Street.

The cold feels good against my eye. I scrounge around the bottom of my bag and come up with a yellow and an orange pill, Vs carved into their chalky faces, their colors signaling how many milligrams. I don't remember which is which.

On the way back to the train, Harold is in front, Letty follows behind him, and I bring up the rear. As cold as it is there is no wind, so it feels mild. Like last night, no one is around, and the streets of Canarsie, Brooklyn, are remarkably still.

Not even the strays are out yet, their eyes filled with warmth that is neither warranted nor returned.

We walk for a long time but don't speak. I keep my eye on Letty's suede coat with its fur trim. My preference is for people who don't say anything when there is nothing to say. After a while, I don't even hear their or my own footsteps. They become part of the silence.

At the station the train screeches to a stop. My mouth fills with cotton, and my eyelids comfortably droop.

Harold knocks me in the arm with his shoulder and laughs. Letty glimpses at us but there is no expression in her eyes. Her head tucked, she dives forward.

In our seats, we all three stare at a billboard whose advertisement is no longer visible through the webbed scrawls, smelling the exhaust and waiting for the doors to fold shut on the empty platform.

We Have Arrived At The End Of The White Man's Rule

Dear Charlie

I clipped a newspaper item in the *Times* about the sailors' race riot in Dunoon that you told Daddy about (enclosed here). It must have been such an odd sensation to walk through the town just afterward. I'm so grateful you didn't walk into the middle of it with Mia and that neither of you were hurt.

Racial violence continues to plague the States as well, with the larger cities manifesting the racial and class unrest of our nation. I'm sure you read about Watts. On TV you could watch parts of the city burning in large and small fires, and in the days following see the charred remains of buildings moldering, turning to ash. The violence has an inevitability about it. I am hopeful that as bad as it is, the destructiveness is a means to building a much different world, where women and people of color don't languish at the bottom of the heap.

There are filthy wrongs in our country of which people are just becoming conscious. The black power and women's movements, and the protests against the war are challenges to the elite class, who have no other purpose than to protect a financial system designed by and for them to prosper. *Their* pursuit of happiness is what they mean when they quote the Declaration of Independence. People of color and women and the poor are to be managed, sent to die in Vietnam, forced to have children they do not want, and paid miserably. But all reigns flourish and die, and I believe we have arrived at the end of the white man's rule.

I know that dad told Mia, and probably you and Eileen, that I think all men are chauvinist pigs. Not true. My perspective is more nuanced than that. Although your race and gender bestows on you a certain privilege, *you* are not part of the ruling elite. People in our country are loathe to talk about class, but it is the defining issue, more so than race and gender. It's not enough to get a scholarship to Harvard, like Barbara did. One must also be plugged in, connected to alumni and business leaders and deans. One's father and grandfather must have known Presidents and CEOs, passing favors from one generation to the other, like kings. We don't come from that sort of blue blood, nor does anyone we know.

It would be laughable if it weren't so sad that we fancy ourselves such a democracy, when there is so little mixing between the races and classes in our country. Even crime, of all things, is not color or class blind. We rape and murder people from our own race and socioeconomic background, contrary to the image of roving black men out to rape the white man's female property. Segregation is more complete than anyone would have imagined.

I don't know when you'll next be able to get leave and visit, but you'll find the States changed from when you were last stationed overseas. In retrospect, there was still a lot of the 1950s during most of the 60s, a naiveté and a belief in changing the course of events through the protest and the courts. Now, there is a different vibe. Revolutionary. It is an amazing feeling to be part of such wholesale change, living history in such an immediate sense, with no need to wait and see how it turns out. It *is* turning out. Now. In the courts, the academy, *and* in the streets.

Before you are transferred again, I would like to visit you in Scotland. I'd love to see Mia before next Christmas. Maybe for her birthday? Eileen told me you live right on the boardwalk. How wonderful it would be to vacation by the seaside before facing another deathly hot summer in New York. Mid-August, I have an interview to clerk for a Supreme Court Justice in Atlanta. I have never interviewed for a job before, and Ma thinks it's too far away. She's says I'll be lonely and keeps asking me how I'll take care of myself. Daddy keeps saying that he doesn't know what he'll do with her if I move away, like you and Carol. That she'll worry night and day. But if I'm going to have a career in law, Atlanta would be a good place to start. There's an opportunity to help shape the Civil Rights law being written there, or at least participate in some way.

Let me know what you think about a visit.

My love to little Mia and Eileen,

Pammy.

I Would Prefer Her Friendship

"Ma, it's Mia," I yell, putting my palm over the receiver.

"What?" she squawks.

I look sideways at her from the phone table in the dining room. My small mother is even smaller these days than the 5 feet she has been for most of her life, except for her beach ball stomach. She lives propped up on pillows on the living room pullout. Her skin thin and ashy gray, but mostly unlined at eighty-nine.

The commercials are on, and the higher decibels make the walls shake.

"She has the TV up so loud because she can't hear anything," I tell Mia. "Not even the TV. I sit next to her and tell her what they're saying on her stories."

Today, it's a Matlock repeat that we've seen maybe twice.

"How is she?" Mia asks.

"So-so," I say. We both laugh. It is all my mother has said for years. "So-so," sing-song-y, though not reminiscent of song. Her fuck you to the world.

"How are you?" Mia asks.

"Women come in and help us," I say. "They're all Dominican with this new place. They're much nicer than the Americans we had before. Last week, one of them found a piece of dirt the size and shape of a pea in grandma's belly button."

There's no response on the other end of the line. I take a drag on my cigarette, the fine web of phlegm in my throat contracts, releases.

"Are you still there?" I ask.

"Yes. That's awful. I guess she's not bathing? Don't they help with that?" Mia asks.

"They mostly give her sponge baths. I guess they missed it."

The three of us, my mother, me, and the young, beautiful Dominican woman had all stared at the pebble of dirt in the aide's palm, relieved that it came out in one piece and wasn't attached to something inside.

"Pammy, it's starting," my mother yells from the living room.

"I should go," Then I remember. "Could you find some out-of-print or rare books? Someone told me it was easy now, with the Internet."

"Yeah, sure."

I give her the names of two Iris Murdoch novels.

"Talk soon," Mia says.

It's not her voice that falters, but something in her that I hear in her voice, if I listen. I don't usually. There's nothing to say anymore. About any of it.

"Pammy!"

"Coming!" I begin to cough. The deep, hurtful mouthfuls of stale air cannot reach my lungs, and my chest and ribs buck.

My throat is like a clogged drain with thick, dirty clots of hair and scum. Once I'm able to take a breath, I sit for a minute. My hand reaches for my throat and chest, the gesture recognizable to me as something automatic that I do after each coughing fit, catching myself or maybe trying to contain parts of myself. My heart and breath.

"Pammy, what's wrong?" my mother yells.

"Hold on, Ma, I'll be right in."

It's not a wish for death, but a wish to have never been born at all.

When Mia was a teenager, she and I knowingly quoted Artaud to each other, not realizing how much we meant this, and what that might mean for our lives. Not that it has meant the same thing to each of us, the delineation being that Mia functions in the world and I do not. I stopped and Mia continues.

"I am a mentally ill person. I will never be a lawyer or a teacher or a writer. It has been years since any of this was even possible. Don't ask me anymore."

It was a relief to say this. I was forty-three, Mia twenty-three. In the intervening twenty years, there has been the weekly phone call, not always as uneventful as they are now. There have been times when she's boycotted me and hasn't called for months, saying I'm verbally abusive. And other times when I couldn't speak or would sob. There are limits to what I can expect of people. And Mia, who wishes she was never born, probably has more limits than most. There's always love in her voice when we speak, but it's shot through with disappointment and disgust: the well person calls the ill one *out of love*. I would prefer her friendship.

A few bars of histrionic theme music emit from the tiny TV speaker. I turn and alternately wheel and scoot my wheelchair, whose left wheel is pigeon toed, always pulling inward, next to the TV tray at my mother's side of the bed. An ashtray the size of a dinner plate teeters on its edge with a tower of smoldering cigarette butts. I douse it with my coffee until it looks like a thick soup. The Dominican women usually cross themselves when they pass the ashtray. On their way out the door.

Neither of us can make it up the stairs anymore. My knees and my mother's back are too weak to hold us, not to mention my emphysema. We sleep together on the pullout couch that just stays pulled out, hogging up the living room. The mattress is so thin it curls at its edges. I'm a lot heavier than my mother, and each night she slides into the depression I create in the bed, and rests against my back. Our touching reminds me of when I rode cross-country on a bus when I was nineteen, and the stranger in the seat next to me and I would fall asleep on each other. It happened at night and during the day we never mentioned it.

I make it back from the kitchen and to my mother without the errant wheel getting caught in the leg of the pullout mattress, whose only real strength is gravity.

I start to interpret. Not verbatim, just "he says she says and now he's going to that guy Sterling's house." I summarize.

My mother breathes heavily and smells sharp and rotten. Her once dark brown eyes are drab and her mouth is permanently tugged down.

My father has been dead for over a year now. It was my sister

Carol's idea to move me back into my parents' house. Or Carol and her accountant's idea. They divvied up all of my father and mother's assets between her and my brother Charlie so that my mother will qualify for a room paid for by Medicare and not by the assets, in three years' time. Well, two now. With the help of the Dominicans we've survived one.

It's not the worst setup. Neither my mother nor I could exist without my father alone. He was our maintenance man.

My mother shakes her coffee cup at me. "Pammy," she says, like I'm halfway across the room. "I finished my coffee."

"All right," I yell back, like I'm on the other side of the room. "Hold on a sec."

I realize when the end of the show theme music plays that it is only ten in the morning, with two more *Matlock*s, and an old movie on Channel 5, around noon.

The realization of the hour is a burden. The Dominican woman doesn't come until one on Sundays, and then just stays for two hours, to tidy up and make us dinner. Her limited presence is set off like parentheses, apart from us, whereas on the other six days she's here for eight hours, nine to five. There's solace in the extended amount of time she's here, as if most of the day will be helped along somehow, dealt with, by someone else.

"Are you getting my coffee?" my mother asks. She doesn't look at me, but keeps her eyes on the rolling credits.

"Yeah, I got it, Ma."

I place my mother's and my coffee cups in my lap and begin my lurching way into the kitchen, which smells singed. The stubborn wheel hits the table and I back out to coax it forward, to the extent that it will cooperate, which isn't that much, but enough to get to the counter. The coffee is inky and lukewarm. Condensation streams down the inside of the glass carafe. It's an old coffee maker, its white plastic long ago having yellowed then browned, thoroughly cooked. My parents have never been the kind to replace things. My father spent the last twenty years of his life repairing and scrubbing clean toasters and countertops, linoleum and carpeting, so that the house appears unhappily preserved.

I pour what's left of the coffee into my cup and start a new pot. The element hisses, and a belch of steam escapes from the lid.

"I'm making a new pot, Ma," I yell. I doubt she hears me, but it is one of those rare moments when she is all right to be on her own in the living room or she'd be screaming for me.

I light a cigarette and take a sip of the coffee turned to sludge. The acrid smell of the kitchen coats my tongue, sticks in the back of my throat.

On the window's ledge, one of the squirrels expertly rotates an acorn around and around, stripping its glossy shell. Her tail twitches and her eyes do a quick scan of the neighbor's tree, whose leaves and nuts fall into our cement backyard, bordered by hardened strips of soil where no one ever decided to grow anything. The squirrel is preparing to jump to the ground for another nut, then return to her safe perch, her body alive with industry, with fight. I've watched her, and others like her, before.

I forget who it was who said that it was cowardly to envy animals. From his perspective (and I would wager that it is a man), I am a profound coward. I envy not only animals, but flowers and clouds. Things that are alive but whose nature is not to reflect on their progress in time.

The beginning theme music starts up. I imagine Andy Griffith's face on the screen, and my mother's face, turned to his. She is interested in him in a way that she is not with actual people.

"Pammy, Pammy," she cries out.

"Coming." I pour our coffee. I will have to take my mother's in first, then mine, or it'll all spill.

"Pammy, it's on," she yells.

Me and my bum wheel hurry in. The coffee sloshes in my lap, forming a little see-though spot on my pajamas.

The show has begun. Matlock gets wind of something or other, and he's off wherever the scent takes him.

"Here, Ma."

"Good." She lights another cigarette.

I LOOK AT HER INTENT eyes, following Matlock, getting her bearings. Which episode is this?

My mother doesn't remember having my father kneel to clean the floor, making him go down and up, to and from the basement, washing their falling apart clothes and towels, during the last two years of his life. He had bone cancer, would've been in great pain. This, no one knew until afterward, when my brother Charlie had an autopsy done. But my mother doesn't remember being told about daddy's bone cancer, either. Or threatening to kill me or my sister, or trying to kill me, I think that's what she was doing anyway, or what she might've done, all those years ago on the second floor.

"Pammy, is this the one where his cousin is found dead in the river?"

"Yeah yeah, that's right. I'll be right back, Ma. I'm going to get my coffee," I say, turning my chair.

It's her absence of memory against our word. Where does it leave us all? Is it like only part of it happened if she no longer remembers, and we're alone with our memory of her? I don't know.

In the kitchen, behind the grimy face of an electric clock, it is ten-fifteen. I pour my third cup of coffee. The squirrel is gone when I look for her. I hear Matlock talking to a woman. My mother yells, "Pammy, Pammy, where are you?" like I might have left, when we both know otherwise.

It Has Always Been So

I WAKE UP NOT KNOWING where I am. The room rocks gently. I puzzle over a squat figure standing against the wall, until it formulates properly in my mind and eye as a sink. I realize that I'm not in my own bed, and a sensation like falling overwhelms me in the moments before I catch myself. I'm in Scotland, visiting Mia and my brother and Eileen. The sky through the window is thick and soupy, a grayish color. My mouth is dry, my tongue inert and swollen, like something lying wounded inside a cave.

CHARLIE PICKED ME UP IN Glasgow last night around eight, which seems like a long time ago now.

"A few too many vodkas." The stewardess smiled, and handed me over. She was tall and capable, and I was drunk and at eye level with the pair of tiny golden wings pinned to her lapel, the marigold color all the more prominent for the sea of blue uniform on which they soared.

"Thank you," Charlie replied.

"It's the altitude and the booze. They're used to it," he said, as we watched the stewardess walk away. There was no tone or an expression that accompanied his statement to help define what he meant. Embarrassed? Indifferent?

I used to think his blankness had an aim, or that it stood for a certain reserve. But I think expression just doesn't come naturally to him. You'd think he was holding a cracked dish of a face together, or that he had a head full of rotten teeth to hide. Probably, his stillness is a mask concealing the pain that normal people learn to hide so as not to dwell, as my psychiatrist would say. I am not normal, he would also point out. I am defenseless against dwelling. A behaviorist, my psychiatrist always implores me to examine the thoughts that lead to the suicidal feelings. There is no thought, I've told him. Just feelings. *They* dwell, I insist. In me. Why would I want to dwell in them? That doesn't make any sense! My psychiatrist obviously sees a connect-the-dots diagram when I sit across from him. What he doesn't understand is that thoughts don't assail me; they soothe me. It's the feelings that arrive unannounced, from a place inside, where they dwell. It has always been so.

As Charlie and I walked to the escalator and then to the luggage carousel, I wondered if the people passing us realized on some animal level that he wore a mask and I did not? They might, I decided. People know a lot. They don't know everything, like what the mask hides away. Nor do they care to know this.

For me, watching Charlie's held-together face is always like looking at the shadows beneath the water's surface to violent beatings from my father, after which he ran away for days at a time. My father never hit, or even disciplined me and Carol. We were considered my mother's domain. Charlie was my mother's great love. When he ran off she would not speak to my father or Carol or me during his absence. She mourned him. When I was five, six, and seven, those three or four days invariably felt like being trapped under a collapsed building, unable to breathe, until Charlie came along to lift me, us, out from the rubble. Those airless days also had a dangerous feeling. What if he never came home? My mother might kill us. And of course eventually he didn't come home. He enlisted in the Navy when he was seventeen. Already, Carol was in the convent by then. I was eight years old and alone. I felt like I was being walked around the house blindfolded, my mother always pointing me in the wrong direction, hoping I'd step onto a precipice and to my death. My father quietly watching. Wordless.

"ARE YOU ALL RIGHT? YOU want some coffee?" Charlie asked while we waited for my luggage. The empty conveyor belt clanked past. All of us passengers stood three lines deep, exhausted and staring at the black ribbons out of which our suitcases would eventually tumble.

Charlie explained that Eileen and Mia had stayed behind in case my flight was delayed or we missed the last ferry to Dunoon, and had to stay in the city with Eileen's sister.

"Mia cried like I'd told her she could never leave the house again when I told her she couldn't come. She's at an age. I feel sorry for her mother," he said, like he didn't also live with the two of them.

It was just getting dark when we left the airport. I don't re-member what, if anything, we talked about. It's possible we said nothing, or very little worth remembering. We passed a succession of Glasgow tenements with spiked, punitive fencing. Even the lights glinting through the windows lacked warmth, seemed to signal only how cold and dim their hallways were.

Charlie was directed onto the ferry by someone clad head to toe in yellow raingear, beaded wet from the ocean, faceless from our perspective, all arms.

After Charlie turned off the car engine, we stepped onto the deck briefly. Our hair violently whipped around our faces, and the few words we yelled into each other's ears were lost to the wind. The ferry started to move and my stomach clenched.

"I'll be right back," I yelled, pointing. I ran toward the bottom of the stairs.

In the closet-sized bathroom, I threw up and had diarrhea simultaneously. I kept thinking I should feel raw pain in my throat and ass. But I did not. The spewing was effortless. Apt. *This is life, fleeing your body.*

I cleaned my face, neck, and the front of my shirt with freezing tap water. Head-to-toe, my flesh smarted with the cold.

Back in the car, Charlie lit a cigarette and offered me one.

"I'll get you a couple of cartons from the base before you leave," he said.

I pinched a Kent cigarette between my fingers, recalling the packaging as Eileen's brand. In tandem, we leaned forward and cracked our windows. The cold air and the smoke washed against my face, waking me up a little.

"Does Mia like it here any better?"

Charlie exhaled. "No. I don't think so. She's waiting to go

home, she tells anyone who asks, and even when they don't."

Mia is twelve, and I haven't seen her in two years. She's only ever been to New York for a couple of weeks each year since she was born, always over Christmas, when the displays at Lincoln Center and in shop windows tell enchanting stories with lights and giant Santas and reindeer. There's nothing quite so grand in Dunoon or in Glasgow, I know from my visit two Christmases ago.

"We won't make it home for the holidays this year, but I've put in for a transfer," Charlie continued. "I should get my orders in the next couple of months. Probably San Diego, but maybe upstate New York."

"That's great," I said.

He nodded. "The base is transferring a number of subs. I'd rather ask to leave than be told I'm going to Guam or Germany."

"Where upstate?"

"Albany. They need a recruiter up there."

"How does Eileen feel about that?" I asked.

"Not happy. She's made a lot of friends here. And leaving her sister will be really hard."

"Um."

"She's always known that the plan was to go back to the States, though," he said, flicking his ash into the wind, probably justifying the move with the memory of long ago statements and agreements. As if people mean what they say, or even remember what they thought about and said twelve years ago.

As we drove off the ferry and entered the small town, I realized that Dunoon had been contained in my memory only as one scene, the boardwalk and the ocean. But there were a lot of narrow, steep, and hilly streets that I'd totally forgotten about, all of them from a harrowing perspective, as if they'd jumped from the mind of a visual artist and onto a cramped page. Before we plunged down one such street, Charlie pointed at a toy shop and said the sailors had destroyed the entire store during the riots.

"There were dolls all over the place, lying around in the broken glass. The Navy paid for all the damage."

"What happened, anyway?" I asked.

"A Scotsman said something to one of the black sailors, and he went back to the ship and got a bunch of his friends. They don't like us here, never have," he shrugged. "I'm just glad we didn't walk into the middle of it."

I nodded, imagining Charlie and Mia finding the dolls' unperturbed expressions on beds of shattered glass.

When we got to Charlie's apartment house, Gowan Bank, we heard Joan Baez's "The Night They Drove Old Dixie Down." Charlie and I slammed the car doors. A rustling of talk and laughter gathered in the narrow, concrete alleyway that we followed to the front entrance. The murmuring ribboned from the open windows and door. People stood and also sat on the stairway with drinks in their hands, as we made our way up to the second floor. Navy couples lived on the first and third floors, so there were no neighbors who were not out here somewhere, no one to complain about the noise. Everyone said hello, looking down or up at me. They asked how my trip was. Inside, the apartment was totally packed, the din was no longer murmurish, but struck me viscerally, in waves.

Mia ran toward me from a crowd of kids, screaming, "Aunt

Pam!" She was still on the small, skinny side for her age, but everything else about her had changed. Her face had definite personality, a direct gaze that held a warmth and curiosity that other people seemed to lack.

One of the kids in the circle she'd just left called her name.

"Okay," she said over her shoulder, rolling her eyes at me.

She wore a white leather miniskirt with boots to match, and a shiny red top. As she pulled away slightly to look at me, a small silver bracelet danced up and down her arm as she tucked her hair behind her ear, a universal move of pretty girls everywhere. Mia was very pretty now, like Eileen and her side of the family. Unlike ours. But she still resembled our side, her dark hair and eyes. I wished I could ask her to stand still, so I could study her and trace all the ways in which she had changed. But I knew better. I wondered if she would still like me, now that she was growing up.

"We're going outside, you wanna come?"

"Let your aunt relax for a minute," Eileen said, placing a Manhattan in my hand. Mia looked at me pointedly, not frowning but insistent, like we were an old married couple.

"We'll talk later," I said. "We have a lot of catching up to do."

Eileen hugged the two of us, her drink spilling a little onto the shag carpet. A warm drunken smile bumped into my ear.

"Welcome," she said.

The pink and green geometric pattern of Adair Sacuba's catsuit-tunic swarmed toward us. Adair and I had become friends the last time I visited, smoking pot on the beach almost every night after dinner and talking about prehistoric matriarchal societies and feminist theory. She was one of the only Navy wives I'd met who'd graduated from college. She had also worked for a publishing house before she got married. Somewhere in Seattle, where she met her seal: Slick Willie, she called him after a few drinks, which was most of the time.

Amazonian, Adair towered over most of the men and all of the women in the room. Her hands raised in the air, she yelled,

"Pammy, you're the shit." With a pixie haircut and large hoop earrings, she leaned in, whispering, "Get your ass in the ocean, it helps with jet lag, hon." She pointed an unlit cigarette at me.

"I'm having a shindig at my house tomorrow night and I don't want you to sleep through it."

Adair pinched the cigarette between her lips and looked around for a light. Leaning into the crowd and over Mia's head, she reached for someone's lit cigarette, igniting her own. Having bumped into Mia seemed to remind her that she was there.

"Look at you. You look like one of the Top of the Pops girls in that getup."

"Twelve going on twenty," Eileen said.

"I'll be outside," Mia said, looking at me, satisfied that there was something of ourselves that we would share only with the other. I'm nine years younger than her parents, and younger still in her eyes because I don't have children. I'm nobody's mother, and Mia is opposed to mothers and parents. It's her age, as Charlie said. Or maybe it's an intuited sense of herself and what she thinks of the world. I wouldn't be surprised. In one of her letters she included a story about a little girl who'd gestated in a pod that gently seesawed from a tree branch. No parents. She grew up in the forest whose trees had edible bark that tasted of whatever she wished, and returned to her pod to sleep each night. The crude drawings that accompanied the story managed to get across a sense of freedom. The main character was not afraid, but unencumbered with heritage.

I hadn't drunk a Manhattan since my last visit. I looked at the cherry at the bottom of the smoky amber colors. "Cheers," Eileen said, bumping into the bar globe so that all the bottles clinked in their separate holders. Maybe it was the jet lag or the lack of sleep and food, but as soon as the liquor hit my belly I was drunk again.

One of the last things I remember from last night was the shock of cold before my limbs turned numb in the black water. Adair and I held hands over the waves, until they lifted us into the sky. People from the party lined up along the rocky shore, screaming at us to come back. One of them angrily crashed through the foam, toward us.

"Jesus Christ the two of you are going to drown." Even in the dark, I could recognize Adair's husband, his eyes bulging from his large, block-shaped head. He grabbed her arm, then mine, yanking. "Get off me you asshole," I yelled. My arm slipped from his fingers and I was alone. I let the current carry me past the breakers. People waved from the shore and I waved back. I don't remember the rest. How I got to bed. Or undressed. Under the covers I see that I'm wearing a large white nightgown, not my own. For a couple of seconds, I feel like I'm spiraling again, only now I know where I am. But still. I don't feel like I'm somewhere. I could be anywhere is how it feels.

ALL THE TIME SINCE I first woke up not knowing where I was—it must be a couple of hours at least—I thought I was just lying here thinking. But I must've slept, too. The sky is light now, and the gulls' high-pitched calls have joined with the ocean's sloshing. The shoebox guest room is made to seem even littler with patterned wallpaper and wall-to-wall carpet, like its gift wrapped from the inside. Glass doors open onto a tiny veranda, overlooking the impressive yard that flows from the front entrance to the boardwalk to the sea.

The bedroom door nudges open and Mia's head pops in. Her cat zips from between her feet.

"Hi Aunt Pam!" she says, launching herself onto the small bed so that she lands with a whap. The cat springs up after her and walks on my hair. Without the miniskirt and boots, the delicate bracelet, Mia looks more like the younger Mia that I remember. More like a child than a small adult in her pajamas. I'm relieved at this.

I smile, trying to ignore the hangover pressing in at me. "Hi Mia. And this must be Gypsy?" I say, turning to the large black and white cat.

"He follows me everywhere," she says. "He's really my cat," she continues, stroking him. "He steals the fishermen's catch if we let him out too early, and they chase him with bricks and poles. So we have to keep him in in the mornings."

"Didn't he kill a seagull, too?" I ask, remembering something Eileen once told me.

Mia's eyes widen. "Mom had to go out with a broom to get the whole flock away from him. We could see them diving at him out the window. I was screaming, it was horrible."

I think of what Charlie told me yesterday, about moving back to the States. How they'd either have to quarantine Gypsy or give him up. Either way, Mia will be devastated. Gypsy, too. I watch him watch her, like they're peers and in this together. He kneads my shoulder and Mia climbs under the covers. The large rainbow-patterned bedspread ripples, and ice cold air slaps my bare legs. Mia doesn't put her head on my shoulder as she did two years ago. Our bodies don't touch at all. Instead she looks up at the ceiling, pulling the covers under her chin. Gypsy walks over my chest and curls up next to her face, between us. I haven't had a cat since Tao disappeared last summer. Waiting for him to return home became a habit, and then hesitancy took hold. Or an aversion, maybe, to getting and losing another cat.

What I know of Mia's life here is the broad outline, meaning I know something of the important details, but I don't really know how she feels about the things she tells me. She is such a verbal, theatrical child. Something of her is lost in the monthly letters, and even on the phone. What I do know from her correspondence is that she wears a uniform to school and that she hates the uniform and the school. That she steals her mother's smokes and got so drunk at the Fourth of July party at the base that she passed out and threw up all over herself. Some of the kids she was with thought she would swallow her tongue and die. This, she told me as if she'd earned a great distinction among her tribe as a result of her near-death due to drunkenness. One of the kids threw her in the pool to clean her off and wake her up. Afterward, she ran around soaking wet all night and no one noticed.

"The parents were all drunk off their asses," she wrote, with a number of exclamation points. Mia wants me to meet this kid, Kathy Parely, the one who dragged her to the pool.

"She's from California," she told me, an indication of her singular Americanism, the height of which Mia can never hope to attain, with her mother being from here. Showers are also alluded to with great reverence. "I need a shower," she wrote in her last letter. "A hot shower instead of a cold bath in dirty water."

THE OCEAN GROWS LOUDER. RAINDROPS fly against the glass doors.

"Let's go to Jean and Effie's for breakfast," Mia says looking over at me, the small motion enough to disturb the cat. He rises and looks over the side of the bed, thinking about jumping down.

Jean and Effie own the bed and breakfast next door to Gowan Bank. Mia lives over there as much as she does here. She helps set and clear the tables on the weekends. The women feed her chocolates and the three of them watch *Upstairs Downstairs*, Mia has mentioned, when they babysit her every Saturday night.

"That's fine with me," I say. "Will your parents mind?"

I want to be mindful of Charlie and Eileen. I've heard through my mother that they're worried about my influence on their only child.

"They're sleeping in," she says. "They always do after a party."

"What time is it anyway?"

"Seven-thirty. Do you remember last night?" she tries, experimentally.

"I was in the ocean," I say, closing my eyes. It feels so good to close them. I wish I could just lie here all day, listening to the waves.

After stepping around on my hair, and not jumping from the bed, Gypsy lies down, pulling my scalp taught. I try not to move.

"They had to go get you," Mia says. "Fish you out of the ocean, that's what someone said. And you were singing," she continues, more and more enthusiastic in the telling. "The Melanie song." She strokes the cat and he purrs loudly.

"I don't remember any of that, especially not the singing," I say, looking over at her.

"Everyone thought that was really funny, but Mom and Dad were worried. My dad started to yell at people, saying not to laugh. He got a bunch of people to drag you out."

"Was your dad mad?" I ask, regretting having drunk so much yesterday.

"No," she says shaking her head. "I don't think so. Just worried. He saw a drowned guy once, so he freaks when people go swimming at night. They do it a lot at our parties," she shrugs.

I have to go to the bathroom, but the thought of stepping from the bed and to the outside hallway, where the shared bathroom is located, keeps me pinned to the spot of warmth that Mia, the cat, and I have generated.

Outside it starts to pour.

"It's always rainy here, and cold, especially in the mornings," Mia says wearily. "Kathy Parely says it never rains in California."

"I guess that's true," I say. "But you're not a West Coast personality. You're definitely an East Coast personality."

"I am?" Mia asks, interested to hear my assessment of her.

"I went to a party in Los Angeles once and all the people from New York were in one room talking and drinking, and Californians were in another, smoking dope and lying around on the floor. You'd be in the New York room."

"Well, I was born there."

I smile at the sound of her grown-up voice.

"In the same hospital as me."

"I wonder what it's like to be born? I wish I could remember. It seems important," Mia says. She stops petting the cat and flops down on her back, staring at the ceiling again.

"There's something called rebirthing. Probably they do that in California. A therapist makes you hyperventilate, and somehow this enables you to go back through time, to your birth," I say.

"That is so cool," Mia says.

"How do you get up in this cold?" I ask, still not wanting to disturb the little bit of warm air under the covers. A gnawing headache has begun to bore into the space between my eyes, the hangover no longer threatening, but here.

"I usually have all my clothes laid out on school days, and I change under the covers."

"What about on the weekends?"

"I run to the bathroom with the blankets around me and stand in front of the heater in there until the water runs hot," she says.

"Be careful, with the blankets and the heater," I say.

"I am," she says, and I remember that I did not tell my brother about the Fourth of July drinking because Mia is a cautious child, in general. It was uncharacteristic of her, I thought, the little girl who turns all the lights out when they're not being used and cleans up after her parents' parties. Maybe she just wanted to find out what drinking was like, seeing everyone she'd ever known was drunk half the time.

"I'll get up first," she says as if we've been debating who will venture out into the freezing air first.

"Fine with me," I say.

Mia and the cat jump from the bed. The sound of steady rain underscores the desolation loose in the room now that I am alone. This sense is so palpable it seems that it exists in the room itself. Its walls and the ceiling.

The gulls' cries have died. I imagine them perched on the stone fences all along the front yards, their heads tucked into their wings, taking a beating.

It's not satisfaction I feel but something like that, when the headache starts to pulse in one of my eyes. Hangovers so aptly define punishment, which seems warranted, not for drinking, necessarily. But for feeling so wretched. It is punishment, and cause for punishment, all in one.

"I'm done, if you want to use the bathroom," Mia says, standing at the side of the bed. I must've fallen asleep again. Mia looks slightly worried, like I might disappoint her. And if it weren't for her, I would never get out of bed until the afternoon on my visits to Dunoon. I'd wait until the heaters and fires had been roaring for a number of hours, and it was time to drink again.

"Good Morning!" Jean says when we enter the bed and breakfast foyer. It's small and dark and not appreciably warmer in here than it is outside.

"I hope you brought your appetites," enjoins Effie. "It's a good thing you're here, Aunt Pamela," she says, bumping my shoulder. This one's on about you nonstop."

"I told her about your writing," Mia says in explanation. "And that you were on David Frost."

"On the telly!" she says, shaking her head. "And your speeches. I could never get up in front of people," Jean says, not admiringly, but considering the pain it would cause her.

"It helps to have a drink," I say.

"Aye, that's the way," she says, winking.

"Come girls," says Effie.

We follow the silhouettes of Jean and Effie down an even darker, narrower hallway. Jean is taller than Effie, but they both look like hens, with their protuberant midsections, absent a distinction between their breasts and bellies, followed by skinny calves. Women are called hens in Scotland, not chicks. I had always thought it had to do with being a mother hen, but now I think it may have to do with the henlike shape we eventually assume.

Jean opens a sliding door on a vast and startlingly light room, colder still, as if we'd somehow blundered onto a frozen tundra from the dim portal of a single-file hallway. The room is empty. The twelve tables are perfectly spaced and laid with stiff white linens. The cream wall to wall carpet a riot of open azaleas. Jean runs over to plug in the space heater and shovels coal onto the almost dead fire, while Effie seats us next to the huge bay window. Its steady draft whistles through the old, vibrating panes.

"I'll be right back with some toast and tea to get you started," Effie says, the lace curtains reflected in her small, round glasses.

"Thank you," I say.

Mia and I watch and listen to the rain rhythmically coursing from the gutters, hitting the alleyway between Gowan Bank and the bed and breakfast with a loud slap every couple of seconds.

"It should warm right up," Jean says, struggling from her knees and placing the coal bin to the right of the hearth. I don't think it'll warm right up. It looks more like we'd need to gather round the fire or the heater, like Mia does in the bathroom, to feel warmth in this room.

"I'll go start on your breakfast," Jean says. "Lovely to see you again."

Since I was last here, Jean's husband has died and she has gone gray. Whereas Effie used to live here alone, and Jean came in each day for work, the two women now reside here together full-time. They close for the winters. I imagine them leaving the heaters off to save money, navigating around the huge, empty hotel tightly wound in their bedclothes with big cups of tea.

Jean walks headlong through one door and Effie comes toward us smiling. She lays the rest of the table with jams and butter and teapot so hot steam pipes from its spout and from around its lid.

"How's school going?" I ask when Effie leaves.

Mia reaches for a piece of toast.

"This kid Duncan and his friends always yell at me and Kathy Parely, 'Yankees go home!' I always tell them I can't wait to go back."

"But your mom's from here," I point out. "You're not a Yankee through and through."

"They only care about my dad," she shrugs.

I try to imagine what it's like for Mia living overseas, with a dad who spends most of his waking hours in an American Navy uniform. No possibility of blending in.

"Here you go girls," Jean says, placing plates of hot food in front of us. "Let us know if you need anything else."

I dredge bits of blood sausage and potato scones through the A1 sauce. The taste of smoked ash and grease is thick and delicious in my mouth. The warmth, too, is delicious.

"What about your classes? What do you like?" I ask. I want her to talk about her studies, encourage her. Barbara, who is now conducting gender studies on primates, showed me an article not long ago about how girls lose interest in school around the time they hit puberty.

Mia shrugs. "I like reading. I hate math. I was Anne Frank when we read the play *The Diary of Anne Frank.*"

"Wow. I didn't know that," I say.

"It was just in class," she says, brushing away the idea that she would mention something so trivial. "Anyway, I want to be an actress. So does Kathy. When we grow up, we're going to live together in California."

Mia stabs at her sausage, which comes apart in flakes, bits of gristle glistening from within the deep black color.

"I know a few actors," I say. "The next time you visit, we'll go meet them."

"Really!?" Mia upsets her knife. It rings against her plate, echoes off the walls and becomes yet another sound, along with the falling gutter water and the hiss of the electric heater, the struggling fire that telegraphs the coldness of the room.

"Sure. You can see their apartments, too," I say. "We'll do a tour. You might want to think of starting out in New York, acting. That's where all the theater is."

At twelve, Mia believes that everything she desires lies ahead. She has this idea of herself as huge in the world, not part of the huge world. Eventually, this perception will turn upside down, or right side up. In the ache my body feels looking at her as she talks about the acting career that waits for her to arrive and claim it, I want the world to be what she dreams of it.

The rain finally slows. The world from the bay window looks glum and saturated. Heavy.

"I could live with you in the Village," Mia says.

"You could. You might want your own place after a while. It's small, remember?"

Mia visited with my father once. The three of us, vastly outnumbered by roaches, stood in the tiny room that doubles as an apartment for only a few moments before it seemed as if the air had been used up, and we ran, or so it seemed, purposefully and gratefully, onto Thompson Street.

"And Kathy still might want to come, even though she's from California."

"You could get an apartment together in the Village," I say.

When I was Mia's age, I didn't think of the future beyond getting away from my mother. Which was also a kind of dream.

I realize that I still have to tell Charlie and Eileen that I withdrew my name from consideration for the job in Atlanta. It was after the abortion that I can't tell them about. Charlie, especially, wouldn't understand.

My father took me, and my mother waited for us at a coffee shop.

"You're not fit to take care of yourself," she said to me, like I'd told them I wanted to keep it. It was never a baby to me. There'd never been any question in my mind that I would want to give life to anyone.

My father stayed at my apartment that night. He cleaned and spoke to my mother every few hours, who kept calling to say how it wasn't the right time for me to take a job away from home. "She's right," my father said, washing dishes and killing roaches. "There are plenty of jobs here in New York. There's no one there to take care of you. We worry, Pammy."

I hear a foghorn calling out and watch a battleship move in and out of the fog.

"We can smoke in the alley," Mia says. "Or the close. That's what they call it here," Mia explains, using a Scottish accent, pushing her plate away.

"I like that, it aptly describes the space," I say.

I feel around in my bag for the joint I stashed in the zippered compartment.

As if on cue, Jean and Effie flutter in and begin to remove our empty plates.

"You should come for tea later," Effie says. "Jean's making some butter scones."

I nod my head. "That would be nice. Thank you. It's nice to see you again," I say.

In the close Mia smokes a cigarette and watches me smoke most of the joint before I pass it to her. She expertly pinches it between her thumb and index finger. Her head tilts back like she's laughing. Over her shoulder, I see the only color for miles around, fuchsia blossoms on the azalea bush, blown sideways in the rain and the wind. Pebbles crunch underfoot whenever we shift from one foot to the other. Even though we're barely moving, my ears roar with their sound.

This Particular Minute

"WHERE'S THE PHONE?" I ASK. Mia looks around in the blanket folds and points. I grab the cell phone my sister Carol bought me and look to see if anyone called. No one has called since Carol, on Thanksgiving Day. Carol is alone now, too. I don't know how long it has been since Thanksgiving. Two or three days. Possibly more.

Mia is visiting in between flights from New York to Vermont. Not an earnest visit, but stopping in before I die, scuttling onto a train from JFK to Woodmere then back, on her eight-hour layover. I haven't looked at her since she arrived and I ignore the effect this has. I can tell it has some effect because I can hear the questions and observations that were only moments ago forthcoming dying inside her mouth before being spoken. Out of the side of my eye I see her looking at the closet, at the clothes she and Eileen have sent me over the past year, their tags on them still. Hanging, ghostly. I don't wear clothes anymore, only pajamas that are easy to slip in and out of, to clean. When I die, they will bag up all the sweaters and sweatpants with their tags still on and take them to the Salvation Army. Brand-new. Someone else will wear the ghostly clothes.

Mia has brought chocolate, a couple of small pieces of stained glass to hang at the window, and a plant with small pink buds. I pretend not to notice. Or care. I don't really know if I do care that Mia is here, that she has little gifts that she imagines will brighten the room where three women will soon die. Ugly Phyllis in the bed next to mine pretends she is asleep so she can listen in. The woman in the bed next to Phyllis's, the one closest to the door, is breathing so heavily it makes my chest and lungs scream with anxiety. I suck on the oxygen tank. I say to Mia, "Take me to the nurse's station." Still I don't look at her.

"What do you need?" she asks.

"Take me to the nurse's station."

Mia walks around my chair and pushes me past ugly Phyllis, whose bug eyes I see following us.

"She's a bitch," I say to Mia, staring right at Phyllis. She mouths to me, "You crazy."

The other bed I try not to look at. It's enough to listen to her drowning in her bed.

It's the raging bitch of a nurse called Cindy who stares down at us from the tall barrier that separates the nurse's station from the floor, as they call where we, the dying, live.

"I need my cream," I say to her.

"Let me read your chart," she says, turning to walk off.

"I don't need a prescription for my cream," I say, knowing that once she gets into my chart she will stare and stare at it like a baboon, and tell me she doesn't see anything about a cream.

"My cream, I need my cream," I yell. "What is wrong with you that you can't give me my cream? My legs hurt from the Depends."

"I told you I have to look in your chart," she says, sharp but not looking at me or at Mia.

Mia says, "Does she really need a prescription for that? Isn't it over the counter?"

"Am I talking to you?" Cindy asks.

A word of protest begins in Mia's mouth, which opens and makes a noise.

"Let's go," I say to Mia before she can figure out what it is she wants to say.

"The other nurse will be here at three. She'll give me my cream. Then you can leave."

Back in the room, past the woman drowning and ugly Phyllis, Mia sits down on the edge of my bed again and gravely begins about having me transferred to a Hospice Hospital in the city.

I can hear Phyllis listening.

"I don't want to go," I say to Mia but look at Phyllis, who shakes her head at the air and raises a nostril in a silent growl.

"Don't you think it'll be nicer there?"

"Nicer?" I ask. "No. I don't think that. And hospice comes twice a week."

"But they'd be better equipped to help you. Give you pain medications …" She trails off.

"It doesn't matter. Where's my phone?" I ask. "Could you find it?"

Phyllis turns over, her back to us. I nod my head toward her, and Mia looks at her bed and back like it's the first time she's noticed there's someone else lying there.

She finds my phone on the end table, hands it to me. I check to see if anyone has called. It's still Carol's number, from Thanksgiving Day. Sometimes Carol calls multiple times a week, having forgotten we've already spoken. Then, I won't hear from her for two or three weeks. She lives alone in a retirement condo and doesn't see anyone except a cleaning woman once a week. She gets lost in the days and weeks, forgets where she is.

"What time is it?" I ask.

"Two-thirty," Mia says.

"The other nurse gets here at two forty-five for her three o'clock shift. We'll go back out then."

Mia wheels me out again at the appointed hour. There's overlap between Onny and Cindy. I watch Cindy's nasty face when Onny hands me my cream. She pretends she's reading something, but I can see the little thread of hatred pulling on her mouth.

"And who is this, Pamela?" Onny asks, looking at Mia.

"My niece," I say.

"It's nice to meet you," Onny says. "Where are you from?"

"Vermont," Mia says.

"That's a long way!" she says. "That's nice of you to visit!"

Onny is a warm person in a sea of numb, frozen people. Her eyes twinkle at me and I meet them. They are the only eyes I've looked into for months.

Mia wheels me back, placing me in front of the window where the little pieces of stained glass quiver in the baseboard heat.

Pastoral scenes, a cow with the green mountains behind her, a beautiful rooster.

"You can go now," I say.

Mia touches my shoulder and leans over to kiss me on the cheek. "I love you," she says.

I catch her looking at the hanging clothes again on her way out. Thinking what, I don't know. But something.

She is no longer young at forty-five. I don't know anything about Mia or her life. Just where she lives and what she does, like someone I would meet on a plane. I only know her from the vacuum of the Sunday call. Short and concerned, they've kept on after my mother's death.

In the hall, I listen to her introduce herself to Onny, and I hear Onny say, "Someone will call you."

That's for when I die. Mia is on the list, along with Carol and Charlie.

Sometime soon, relatively soon, soon enough, in the middle of her day or at its end, maybe even at the beginning, the hospice worker will call Mia and say, "Pamela is actively dying," or "Pamela died this afternoon."

I've eavesdropped on the phone call. I know how it goes, and I've always wondered about the first one, the "actively dying" call. Why not wait? Is it so someone, somewhere knows that our feet have turned blue as our blood pools near the vital organs, and our chests buck and our lungs struggle to not be engulfed, finally? Most dying is not peaceful, I've discovered living here. It's loud and violent. I've asked the hospice worker about what I've seen and heard. We've sat here together amiably on the gray afternoons leading up to Thanksgiving, discussing how the body dies.

The next time the hospice worker is here I'll have to ask her about the different phone calls, and if I get to choose who gets which one. If so, I'll tell her I want Mia to know when I'm dying. Charlie and Carol, when I'm dead.

No longer pretending to be asleep, high-pitched whistles and squeals issue through ugly Phyllis's nose and mouth. Her lack of consciousness is a reprieve for me. The woman near the door is also quiet for once. Could be dead, for all I know. The cow and rooster grow warm in the sunlight.

For a couple of minutes, I listen carefully so I can decide when Mia is gone altogether. Is it in *this* particular minute that the double doors to the entrance are slamming shut? I imagine her outside, walking to the train. I have no idea how far it is and how long I might imagine her close to me.

Voices And Laughter Of No One Who Is Present

MIA CALLS FROM SOMEWHERE IN Pennsylvania, where she is at graduate school. I was admitted to St. Vincent's last night. Charlie must have told her to call. The pay phone receiver dangles in the air as the resident who lives closest to the phone lopes off, into his room.

"You were embarrassed by me in front of your friends the last time I visited you in Virginia. You don't care about me anymore," I say.

Noise from the television inside his room is broadcast into the long, blank hallway. "

That's not true," Mia says. "I don't know what to do to help."

"You sound so empty when you talk to me, like there's nothing there," I say.

"I don't know how I'm supposed to sound," Mia says from behind her flat voice. She pauses before she says, "You don't really seem to like it when I call. That's why I haven't called you before this." Another pause. "What happened?"

Charlie probably told her that I was passed out drunk when they found me. Blood everywhere.

"I was mugged and beaten up on the train platform. No one even asked about that. They just wanted to move me out. Human refuse."

"Don't say that," Mia says.

"I expect that from them. That's what madness is to them. An unseemly inconvenience. But I thought you knew better."

Mia is crying now. Hearing her, I begin to cry.

"You don't understand." Mia's voice is raised, cuts toward me through the receiver, no longer impersonal. "I have my own problems. I don't know how to help you. I've tried to help you and I don't know how. I can barely help myself."

"You used to love me," I cry. "When you were little."

"Pamela, you need to get off the phone," the nurse says.

Phone calls are monitored by the staff. They don't want anyone riling us for the rest of their shift. I look over my shoulder at her. She's small and pretty in her youth, probably only a year or two older than Mia is. Twenty-three, twenty-four. She's new here.

"Come on, now," she prompts, smiling a little, tilting her head. She doesn't want a fight.

"I have to go," I say into the receiver.

There are no words for all the hurt I feel about Mia that's not even hurt anymore but hatred.

"I do love you," Mia says.

She has stopped crying, probably listening to the nurse and the sound of the television one door down, how the hallways fill with voices and laughter of no one who is present.

Her words are obscene, her voice harsh and empty.

I wish they'd left me to die.

On the subway platform. Or before that, even. I could have skipped the train platform and Mia's phone call. I don't remember how many times my father has found me slipping away. Three or four. Calling for the help of strangers who've resurrected me like a battery-run car, my veins filling with someone else's blood, my lungs with air. Then the brutal light of reawakening when I wished only to sleep.

Signaling Through the Flames

IT WAS MIA'S IDEA TO open her father's new dartboard. A Christmas present from her. She holds the board out in front of her. The first arrow misses and skids against the picture window. Mia steps backward and trips over a stack of open presents, causing the seven-foot Christmas tree to sway. A sound like hundreds of little glasses being raised in a toast signals a moment when the tree might fall over. The force of Mia's concentration in that moment is palpable, and when it passes and the tree remains upright, she begins to laugh. Everyone else has gone to bed. The dishwasher halts and resumes, cycling. Half of the house is blazing lights: the kitchen, living room, and laundry room; the other half is in total darkness: the bedrooms. About a half-hour ago everyone went to bed and Mia and I sneaked outside and folded ourselves into a construction tube and got high. Mia said that all the neighborhood kids use it for this purpose. Her cat MacDuff followed us, weaving in and out of our bent legs.

Weed and hallucinogens are what Mia and her friends are

into. "I hate drinking. I have like an aversion to it," she told me, petting MacDuff. "Because of my mom and her friends."

Mia is seventeen. I gave her *The Complete Works of Shakespeare* and Artaud's *The Theater and Its Double* for Christmas. She wants to study theater. She loves Sam Shepard.

"No one does family misery better than Shepard," she said, smiling and raising the joint to her lips. It's weird to think that I held Mia at her christening that the little clump lost in a long white gown is the same body that sits here beside me now. A child still, but not purely.

"You'll find Artaud one of us as well," I told her. "He writes about how theater's role in the world is to communicate through primal and metaphysical impulses more than the realist ones."

"That sounds a lot like Shepard," Mia nodded her head. "He's mythical, brutal."

"Hmm. Artaud said actors and audiences should be like victims 'burnt at the stake, signaling through the flames.' "

"That's beautiful," Mia said.

I study her profile for a few seconds. Mia has our coloring. But like her mother, she's striking. It's those high cheekbones they both have, their faces like dramatic carvings.

"It is beautiful, isn't it? He spent nine years of his life in an insane asylum, then died two years after he was released."

I pinch the outstretched joint between my fingers, look at it to make sure it's still going, and smell the sweet burnt smell of the plant.

"Figures," Mia said, shaking her head.

"My mother had me committed to the state hospital when I was your age," I said.

"I didn't know that," Mia said. "Why?"

"She shouldn't have been a mother," I said. "My father and I had to write letters to each other, which the staff read, where he implied that my mother had committed me because I was spoiled. We had to trick them. It was my dad's idea. I really think it was the only reason they ever let me out after six months instead of three years."

"Jesus," Mia said. "That's totally fucked. Why is Grandpa so scared of her anyway?"

"It's something in her. It's why he stopped seeing his family, or she made him. I don't know the particulars. She needs control."

Mia nodded.

"And I think violence is always a part of that for her. Or the threat of it."

It started to drizzle rain then. Looking out, I noticed that MacDuff had left us, and was walking into a small strip of woods. I slipped the roach into my breast pocket and Mia and I shared a cigarette in silence. I looked out at the mud and earthmoving equipment. We were on the periphery of the neighborhood. Most of the homes were dark, save the evenly spaced pools of light from the streetlamps.

"We should probably get back," I said.

"Leftovers," Mia said, smiling.

I DRAIN MY VODKA TONIC and motion for Mia to reposition the dart board. I sense someone behind me at the exact moment the dart leaves my fingers, hitting the outermost ring on the board. I turn. Eileen's wide blue eyes stare at the two of us for a second or so before she says, "I can't believe you still have the nerve to come here, stoned out of your mind the whole time. I've asked you to leave Mia alone. You're not good for her and you know it." She snatches the dart board from Mia's hands.

"What's wrong with you?" Eileen's eyes linger on Mia in disgust.

"That's rich. What about what's wrong with you? Why don't we talk about that for a change?" Mia asks. "How much did you drink tonight, Mom?"

Eileen looks at me as if I'm the one who has spoken.

"Go to bed. Now," she says to Mia, clutching the dartboard.

I throw another dart at the wall next to the picture window, in front of which stands the tree.

"Give me those," Eileen says to me.

Mia laughs. Glancing down, I see an assortment of feathers poking from my fist: three more darts. One, two, three, in various places and degrees of depth along the window frame. The last one dangles, half in, half out before it drops to the floor. A fallen, tiny exclamation point. I can't help myself, I laugh. The tremendous relief in doing so means a bursting sound that makes the two of us laugh even harder. Eileen's eyes bug in warning.

"You're nuts! I knew that from the first time I met you," Eileen says, pointing at me. She turns to Mia: "Get in your room." Her teeth grit and her face crumples like wadded paper.

Mia screams, "I hate you. I couldn't even bring Greg here because you're drunk all the time, so I don't know what you're talking about."

"There's something wrong with her," Eileen says, pointing at me. "And you're going to be just like her. Who speaks to their mother like that? Only someone with something wrong with them."

In the hallway, I see my mother's bow legs, the eternal housedress.

"That's enough," she says, stepping from the dark of the hallway into the living room. "Eileen, shut up."

"Don't tell me to shut up! You're in my house now, and your crazy daughter is turning her against me," Eileen says.

"Fuck you," I say.

Farther down the narrow hall, I see my sister Carol and her husband, Ted. The only people still sleeping, or at least not in attendance, are Charlie and my father. Asleep or pretending to be. That's a real talent in the small ranch-style house, one level, with the four bedrooms jutting off the narrow hallway. Mia has told me she hates this house. She says misery lives in the walls. The light brown wall-to-wall, which covers each room save the kitchen, is the color of quicksand, close and murky.

"Now everyone should go to bed," Carol says, moving forward. Carol is much taller than my mother, which makes it so remarkable each time I see them together that she appears so small standing next to her, frail almost. I'm surprised she spoke at all. Carol's fear of my mother is acute, as if my mother has the power to destroy her with a look or word. I overheard her once tell a nurse that at some point she had to choose between helping herself and helping me. "I went into the convent," she said. It was the closest anyone ever came to admitting what had happened to me, and not even to my face.

"Look who it is," my mother says, turning on her. She withers Carol at once so that she immediately shrinks back into hallway.

My mother snarls, "We were all surprised you even came. Why aren't you with all your rich friends, looking down on us? Isn't that how you usually spend Christmas?"

Carol's husband says, "That's enough of that." I can't see much of Ted except his red, shiny nose. A drinker's nose, full of pores.

"Who asked you?" my mother continues. "You're not part of this family."

Eileen looks at my mother hard, like she's trying to figure something out.

"Why bring them into this? They have nothing to do with your drunken daughter." Eileen points into the air. "She was throwing darts at Mia."

"I was not," I say. Tiredness seems to fill my limbs with heavy sand. I sit down on the window ledge. Mia sits down next to me, as if we're an audience.

"I'm their mother." My mother takes a step closer to Eileen. "I say what goes on with them, not you. I brought them into the world, didn't I? I can do and say what I like with them."

"Not when you're in my house," Eileen says.

No one has ever challenged my mother. The audience is rapt. Mia looks over at me, but everyone else manages to ignore my snorted laughter.

"Come on, Carol," Ted says. "We're leaving."

"You can't leave. It's two in the morning," Eileen says, turning to them.

"Of course we can leave," Ted says, taking Carol by the arm. They do have a car. So.

"Let them," my mother says, waving her arm through the air. "They didn't want to come anyway. Carol's always hated her family, she's always thought she was too good for us. And I've never liked her," my mother says.

"Don't talk like that about your own child! You are under my roof. If you're going to talk like that you'll have to leave," Eileen says.

My mother turns, pushing her way down the dark hallway, past Carol and Ted's red nose. The guest room door opens, slams shut. We listen to her wake my father, telling him to pack. Hurry up, she says. Get our bags ready.

My mother won't fly, so the bus it is from Brooklyn to Virginia Beach. I don't know where she thinks she's going at two in the morning or how. But a few seconds later she bursts from the room. Next, I hear a door bang against a wall, and she wakes Charlie.

"Get up. You need to take us to the bus station."

"What?" Charlie asks. "What do you mean?"

"Howard!" my mother screams.

I turn to watch my father walking toward us, from what's become the feeder hallway, our backstage, and into the light that encroaches into the small foyer from the living room. He has two large suitcases. At seventy-seven he is tall but stooped, especially so with the cases.

"Daddy, you don't have to do this," Carol says. She begins to stroke her neck, something she has done when she's nervous ever since I can remember. She used to get big red splotches all over her chest and face from the constant rubbing. I don't see her enough to know if this still happens.

Ted puts his hand on Carol's arm, pulling her toward their bedroom door. "Come on," I hear him say. Their door closes.

Charlie is up now. He's looking at each of us as if he's found himself somewhere alien.

"What happened?" he asks.

"Convenient of you to have missed everything," Eileen says, walking into the kitchen. Another door opens and closes. Mia's look tells me Eileen's off to the laundry room to drink. "That's where she hides all her booze," she has told me.

"We need you to drive us to the bus station," my mother says to Charlie. She's opened the front closet. She grabs her coat and puts it on over her housecoat and slips on a little pair of cracked leather flats, bent out of shape. Handing my father his coat, she says, "Let's go, we can wait outside."

"I can't drive you to the bus station," Charlie says. "It's not even open."

"We're going whether you drive us or not," she says.

Out they go. Mia and I turn to look out the window and Charlie joins us, watching them stand in the porch light.

"What happened?" he asks, looking from me to Mia.

"Mom and Grandma had a fight," Mia says.

"Jesus Christ, Eileen," Charlie says into the kitchen.

Mia gets up on her knees, straining to see down the driveway. "Dad, dad. They're leaving."

My mother and father are in fact walking under the first of the many streetlights, their shadows large against the concrete.

Charlie is gone. Just like that, the front door and then screen door slamming behind him.

Charlie gets in his car and follows them. All of the car windows are open and we can see him leaning toward the passenger-side window, talking to them, and the two of them walking, staring straight ahead. Finally they stop and he stops. He gets out and puts their cases in the trunk. He opens the backseat and they get in. He drives away with them.

Mia and I look at each other. "I can't believe it," she says.

I can hear Carol and Ted talking. It sounds like Carol is crying. They don't come back out or leave. Their presence at the end of the hallway is palpable. So is Eileen's, in the laundry room, drinking. The cheap doors of the cheap ranch not up to the task of privacy.

"I think I'll go to bed," I say.

"Me, too. I hate it here," Mia says, looking around the living room. "I can't wait to leave."

When I wake up I smell puke. The room, a blueish veiny color from the baby-blue-colored curtains, stinks of it. A greasy breakfast smell seeps in through the bottom of the door, along with low voices. The front door opens, closes. A car pulls away. Carol and Ted, probably.

I can't stand looking at the color of the air in the room. I burrow under the covers, where I more fully notice the vomit smell is coming from my mouth and pores. My throat hurts and I begin to cry. I feel and see things: the large bottle of Jergens hand cream and the pink bathroom at the top of the stairs, the abortions, how many I don't recall, Harold's mostly, and my father waiting for me in the waiting room, me, who will never be anyone's mother, and my own mother, drinking coffee in a shop near the doctor's office, waiting for the two of us at the end of some block and walking ahead of us on the way back to the train, like she's not with us and can't see us, my father looking at the back of her head and then down at me, holding my elbow and saying "Are you all right, Pammy? I can stay with you tonight." "It's okay, Daddy."

After the last abortion I had my tubes tied. I wanted to be alone afterward. My father had stayed on for previous abortions and on bad nights when the police were called. He'd sung to me about Ireland and had read Graham Greene, the only author in my apartment he cares for, but that time I wanted the quiet of an empty space.

I hear the dishwasher drain. The water gurgles through pipes, sucked up and away, and then jerks into another rinse on an endless cycle.

Moving anything hurts so I try to stay still. I cross my arms over my chest as if I am laid out. Dead. Not for the first time, I wonder what it will feel like to be dead, while knowing that I will feel nothing when I'm dead. So I wonder what feeling nothing will feel like, and whether there is a period of time in which you are dead but aware somehow.

If there will be a moment when I feel relief.

Livelihood

We're in the basement of the YWCA, in a rec room with old wooden chairs that kill your ass, and a light bulb that hangs from the ceiling unadorned. Outside it is raining. Loud, the rain is steady on the roof and clearly heard, even though we're a full two floors away. There are about twelve women at the meeting this afternoon. Damp ponchos and shawls and jeans, scream and point at each other, their umbrellas having clattered to the ground, now lying at their feet. I am merely wished away. The lone founding member of The Feminists who still bothers to come to meetings, though this is, I think, my last. I take aim, the ball sounding as if it has cracked in two. Nimbly, for me, I turn and stand next to the pool stick like a warrior. Out of the corner of my eye I notice the crowd involuntarily flinch. A swig of vodka trickles down, into my throat, dribbles on my chin. A dull splash when I tilt the bottle upright. There is a brief pause in the raised voices. The silence offers little relief to the participants of this shitty talking group. Rather, it's like sitting in a thick backwash of ugly words stuck in the air. It turns out everyone wants to talk about only about themselves: the rich, white married women, the rich, white college women, poor white women, the lesbians, the blacks, the Latinos. No one really wants to join together. The lesbians, especially, won't shut the fuck up and hate everyone else. They infiltrated The Feminists. Rebecca Street stopped coming to the group weeks ago, when one of the lesbians screamed in her face that she was one of those homey black women dispensing wisdom and what the fuck did she know of a lesbian woman's experience? "Nothing," Rebecca Street said. "And if you're anything to judge by, I don't want to know nothing."

I thought the lesbians would stop coming to our meetings, and start their own fucking group. But they're here to challenge us, they say, in a tone so condescending that it is hysterically funny to me. The one who started in on Rebecca Street continues on every fucking week. Poker-faced, with a short, pageboy haircut that seems separate but all of a piece with her head, she says that she's upending our assumptions and our ridiculous belief that we can accomplish anything while sleeping with men. "Are you finished?" I used to ask, when I was still running our meetings, like I was about to snatch away her dinner plate. Now, I say nothing, and she sometimes openly says to the others to not pay attention to me. I play pool in the back of the room and drink. I am willfully ignored.

Today's fighting rehashed previous grievances from all in attendance: charges of classicism, racism, and misogyny, and still managed to be newly fucked up with a new strain of personal disclosure that's even more repugnant. A young, white woman in a flowing skirt takes the break in fighting as an invitation, she says:

"I just got my period, so if I begin to cry." She smiles, already crying. I hit one of the the bright red pool balls, producing that satisfying "crack" sound.

"I grew up in a boarding school," she begins. What follows is a detailed account of not only her secondary schooling, but her ancestry, reaching back to Russia during WWI.

"I acknowledge my privilege," she says. I look over at her as she pauses to gather herself, my cue stick poised for a shot. Her mouth trembles and her neck and face turn completely red. "I want to help in the fight to redistribute privilege," she blurts. "I also acknowledge that in sleeping with men, I am complicit in their oppression of women, and I've decided that the only way to be a true feminist is to stop sleeping with them." People clap, like she's given a performance. One of the lesbians rises and holds her arms out, taking the flowing skirt, crying woman into her arms. At that moment, the applause is thunderous.

An influx of members due to a New York Times article about The Feminists caused most of the original members to leave and form their own groups. Now I see that they didn't begin coming to our meetings to join The Feminists. They came with the intent to infiltrate and destroy us. Men aren't the enemy to them. WE ARE. Our very existence and all the words out of our mouths, our theories and our public acts, everything we do oppresses them because they are not married or heterosexual women, not necessarily educated or white or articulate, even. We have been disinvited to our own group. Only I have kept coming, to challenge them, I've screeched at them on occasion. Is it necessary to have divided us up into circumscribed groups?

We're this and that race and class, and we have sex with him or her. There is no discourse, now, that is absent this clutter. The constant chatter about who sees what through which prism, when this is a shortcoming of all people that only time spent together working for a common goal, will remedy. This divisional practice is only destructive, ultimately. I am tired of fighting. My last group. Going, going, gone.

Now, I hurl the pool stick past the embracing women. It doesn't go near them, not really. But still. The crowd descends, many of them? Most of them? Their heavy woolens smelling of the cold and the wet. They spit, yell, and lift me like practiced cops, out of the room, up the stairs, my legs bashing against the steel treads. I cry, my words garbled and phlegmy. Thieves, fucking thieving dyke bitches. Delivered to the sidewalk, my bottle smashes into hundreds of glass shards. I stare up at a Mailbox and a garbage can; human refuse, people walk around me. I don't know for how long before others are lifting me. Someone swaddles me, the blanket like a straightjacket, and I'm lifted again. No siren silently turning or otherwise, but one of the quiet ambulances, advancing at a quick but not speedy pace. I am not hurt or dying, but on my way to St. Vincent's.

"Superficial cuts," the driver up front says into the radio. "Pamela Kearon. Um, we thought you might." I hadn't realized we were stopped until the vehicle begins again, a small tug toward the back doors, in the ambulance bay.

"What day is it?" I ask the man sitting to my left, idly staring down at me.

Like the opening on a ventriloquist's doll, his lips barely move.

"It's Tuesday."

His face and eyes are barren. I think I could move my hand right through him, like in a cartoon.

Tuesdays, tidy Nurse Jean is on. I like her, not for any other reason than that she does her job, whether she likes it or not. I'd guess she does not. I admire people who hide behind good grooming and behavior, since I have a talent for neither. They keep the world going. On some level, even their playacting means they do care, even if it is tied to their livelihood. I have no livelihood to care after, and I am consigned to some other, worse hell than Nurse Jean. That she is able to recognize me and call my name, like I am someone to her, sometimes makes me cry the moment I see her reaching for me as the three of us, me, the driver, and the attendant, whoosh through the back doors of the hospital.

1984

NOVEMBER 6, 1984. I'M AT a party on Bleecker Street. It's a small apartment whose owner I do not know. We were introduced quickly above and around the heads of other people. Her name is Celeste. My neighbor Ruth invited me as we checked our mail this morning, when I told her I didn't have a TV. "Oh, you should come. The more the merrier," she said.

Ruth was a union steward for an orchestra in New Jersey before she retired here, twenty years ago "It goes by in the blink of an eye," she's always telling me. "I stood right there (pointing to Houston Street) with Orson Welles once, talking about a show he wanted to produce. Seems like yesterday."

I could be there or not for this observation. Ruth repeats these couple of sentences often; I think I just happen by sometimes, during her refrain.

People are packed into the small living room, and squeeze in and out of the much smaller kitchen area to refill their wine glasses. I lean against the small sink, clasping my glass to my breast. Celeste has twice asked if I need anything, probably wondering why I'm standing there alone. I shake my head, smile, and look down at the shiny brick patterned linoleum, unable to form actual words. Other people barely notice me, and still others nod and say hello, assuming they must know me. Wine bottles in various states of fullness and cheese bricks and logs crowd the countertops and the Formica kitchen table, whose chairs have been moved to the living room, forming a semi-circle around the television. The people in the chairs talk animatedly about Geraldine Ferraro. "Gerry," they call her. My eyes are continually drawn to the empty space under the table as people move in and out of the kitchen. My glance then moves to the small opening in the kitchen wall, a window into the living room, where Ruth sits on the couch, behind the semi-circle of the people in the kitchen chairs, straining to see around their backs and shoulders. I also watch the backs of people's heads bobbing in conversation that almost drowns out the sound of campaign parties in Washington or clips from earlier in the day, voter interviews on the steps of City Hall. It doesn't take long, an hour only, for Dan Rather to say, "The only question remains is how big a victory it will be for Reagan?" He brings up the electoral map. The people nearest the television stand with their hands over their mouths, staring at all the states that have turned red, a bloodletting. It's funny, not funny ha ha, how aptly the word landslide seems to apply at this moment. It feels as if the ground beneath me shifts and falls away. I drain my glass, set it in the sink. My heart falls when I feel it about to slip from my fingers. I imagine watching and hearing it shattering against the porcelain, but catch it just in time. I push my way through the people in the kitchen. The living room is still packed, but is waiting-room quiet. I lean over, and touch Ruth on the arm.

"I'm going to go," I say.

"Yeah, okay," she replies. "This is a nightmare."

"I didn't think Mondale would win, but this is awful," the woman next to Ruth says.

"Unfuckingbelievable," a man says.

"Who are all these people who voted for him? I don't know anyone who voted for him!" Celeste says.

People have begun to talk again. Their voices are emphatic, rushing in. No one notices when I leave.

Washington Square Park holds a funereal silence, the musicians and performers from earlier shuffle around as if they were lost. It's only 8:15, and the election is over.

Once I'm home, Mia calls from a Mexican Restaurant in Virginia. In the background, I can hear her friends. Louder than members of the party I've just left, with our fifteen, twenty odd years on them. The Moral Majority and Jerry Falwell, Pat Robertson, and the fundamentalists have managed to hobble me with a private despair too raw to face in this moment. Mia speaks loudly, angrily, of primitive mentalities.

"Not now," I say. "I'll call tomorrow."

I hang up on Mia and the sounds of her friends, and turn off the overhead light. The streetlight floods in through the bars on the windows.

Mia lives near a Rock Church, where charismatic Pentecostals speak in tongues, and get born again. Not to mention the military. Men in uniform, aircraft carriers, and battleships; their homecomings and leavings on the news. She hates it there. Her niche is theater and English majors who plan to scatter to New York and Los Angeles once they've finished their degrees.

Every Saturday last summer, Mia and one of her friends attended counter-demonstrations at one of the abortion clinics. Across the road from them people brandished bloody baby dolls and screamed, 'Murderers," at them.

"They are brutal people," Mia said to me once. "They can't win."

But they have won, twice now; resoundingly, like a door closing.

I stopped working in the movement years ago. Too sick. "I am mentally ill," I told everyone who asked. That usually ended the conversation and any other inquiry during subsequent run-ins. At one time, I *was* buoyed at the thought of Mia carrying on in the movement. But she became a young person, and not herself. The young are nothing to me. Even Mia.

I was so certain the first election was a mistake. That people just didn't know what they were doing. Tonight I have clarity.

I crawl under the covers and breathe in the warm, rank smell of wine on my breath. I listen to glass breaking in the streets, far away sounding at first. But then I hear a dull popping sound in the seconds before the light at the edge of alleyway shatters, and the room darkens.

This long life.

This lonely life.

Fomite

About Fomite

A fomite is a medium capable of transmitting infectious organisms from one individual to another.

"The activity of art is based on the capacity of people to be infected by the feelings of others." Tolstoy, *What Is Art?*

Writing a review on Amazon, Good Reads, Shelfari, Library Thing or other social media sites for readers will help the progress of independent publishing. To submit a review, go to the book page on any of the sites and follow the links for reviews. Books from independent presses rely on reader-to-reader communications.

For more information or to order any of our books, visit
http://www.fomitepress.com/FOMITE/Our_Books.html

More Titles from Fomite...

Novels
Joshua Amses — *Ghatsr*
Joshua Amses — *During This, Our Nadir*
Joshua Amses — *Raven or Crow*
Joshua Amses — *The Moment Before an Injury*
Jaysinh Birjepatel — *The Good Muslim of Jackson Heights*
Jaysinh Birjepatel — *Nothing Beside Remains*
David Brizer — *Victor Rand*
Paula Closson Buck — *Summer on the Cold War Planet*
Dan Chodorkoff — *Loisaida*
David Adams Cleveland — *Time's Betrayal*
Jaimee Wriston Colbert — *Vanishing Acts*
Roger Coleman — *Skywreck Afternoons*
Marc Estrin — *Hyde*
Marc Estrin — *Kafka's Roach*
Marc Estrin — *Speckled Vanities*
Zdravka Evtimova — *In the Town of Joy and Peace*
Zdravka Evtimova — *Sinfonia Bulgarica*
Daniel Forbes — *Derail This Train Wreck*
Greg Guma — *Dons of Time*
Richard Hawley — *The Three Lives of Jonathan Force*
Lamar Herrin — *Father Figure*
Michael Horner — *Damage Control*

Fomite

Ron Jacobs — *All the Sinners Saints*
Ron Jacobs — *Short Order Frame Up*
Ron Jacobs — *The Co-conspirator's Tale*
Scott Archer Jones — *And Throw the Skins Away*
Scott Archer Jones — *A Rising Tide of People Swept Away*
Julie Justicz — *A Boy Called Home*
Maggie Kast — *A Free Unsullied Land*
Darrell Kastin — *Shadowboxing with Bukowski*
Coleen Kearon — *Feminist on Fire*
Coleen Kearon — *#triggerwarning*
Jan Englis Leary — *Thicker Than Blood*
Diane Lefer — *Confessions of a Carnivore*
Rob Lenihan — *Born Speaking Lies*
Colin Mitchell — *Roadman*
Ilan Mochari — *Zinsky the Obscure*
Peter Nash — *Parsimony*
Peter Nash — *The Perfection of Things*
Gregory Papadoyiannis — *The Baby Jazz*
Pelham — *The Walking Poor*
Andy Potok — *My Father's Keeper*
Kathryn Roberts — *Companion Plants*
Robert Rosenberg — *Isles of the Blind*
Fred Russell — *Rafi's World*
Ron Savage — *Voyeur in Tangier*
David Schein — *The Adoption*
Lynn Sloan — *Principles of Navigation*
L.E. Smith — *The Consequence of Gesture*
L.E. Smith — *Travers' Inferno*
L.E. Smith — *Untimely RIPped*
Bob Sommer — *A Great Fullness*
Tom Walker — *A Day in the Life*
Susan V. Weiss —*My God, What Have We Done?*
Peter M. Wheelwright — *As It Is On Earth*
Suzie Wizowaty — *The Return of Jason Green*

Poetry
Anna Blackmer — *Hexagrams*
Antonello Borra — *Alfabestiario*
Antonello Borra — *AlphaBetaBestiaro*
Sue D. Burton — *Little Steel*

Fomite

David Cavanag*h— Cycling in Plato's Cave*
James Connolly — *Picking Up the Bodies*
Greg Delanty — *Loosestrife*
Mason Drukman — *Drawing on Life*
J. C. Ellefson — *Foreign Tales of Exemplum and Woe*
Tina Escaja/Mark Eisner — *Caida Libre/Free Fall*
Anna Faktorovich — *Improvisational Arguments*
Barry Goldensohn — *Snake in the Spine, Wolf in the Heart*
Barry Goldensohn — *The Hundred Yard Dash Man*
Barry Goldensohn — *The Listener Aspires to the Condition of Music*
R. L. Green — *When You Remember Deir Yassin*
Gail Holst-Warhaft — *Lucky Country*
Raymond Luczak — *A Babble of Objects*
Kate Magill — *Roadworthy Creature, Roadworthy Craft*
Tony Magistrale — *Entanglements*
Andreas Nolte — *Mascha: The Poems of Mascha Kaléko*
Sherry Olson — *Four-Way Stop*
David Polk — *Drinking the River*
Aristea Papalexandrou/Philip Ramp — *Μας προσπερνά/It's Passing Us By*
Janice Miller Potter — *Meanwell*
Philip Ramp — *The Melancholy of a Life as the Joy of Living It Slowly Chills*
Joseph D. Reich — *Connecting the Dots to Shangrila*
Joseph D. Reich — *The Hole That Runs Through Utopia*
Joseph D. Reich — *The Housing Market*
Joseph D. Reich — *The Derivation of Cowboys and Indians*
Kennet Rosen and Richard Wilson — *Gomorrah*
Fred Rosenblum — *Vietnumb*
David Schein — *My Murder and Other Local News*
Harold Schweizer — *Miriam's Book*
Scott T. Starbuck — *Industrial Oz*
Scott T. Starbuck — *Hawk on Wire*
Scott T. Starbuck — *Carbonfish Blues*
Seth Steinzor — *Among the Lost*
Seth Steinzor — *To Join the Lost*
Susan Thomas — *The Empty Notebook Interrogates Itself*
Susan Thomas — *In the Sadness Museum*
Paolo Valesio/Todd Portnowitz — *La Mezzanotte di Spoleto/Midnight in Spoleto*
Sharon Webster — *Everyone Lives Here*
Tony Whedon — *The Tres Riches Heures*
Tony Whedon — *The Falkland Quartet*
Claire Zoghb — *Dispatches from Everest*

Fomite

Stories

Jay Boyer — *Flight*
Michael Cocchiarale — *Still Time*
Michael Cocchiarale — *Here Is Ware*
Neil Connelly — *In the Wake of Our Vows*
Catherine Zobal Dent — *Unfinished Stories of Girls*
Zdravka Evtimova — *Carts and Other Stories*
John Michael Flynn — *Off to the Next Wherever*
Derek Furr — *Semitones*
Derek Furr — *Suite for Three Voices*
Elizabeth Genovise — *Where There Are Two or More*
Andrei Guriuanu — *Body of Work*
Zeke Jarvis — *In A Family Way*
Arya Jenkins — *Blue Songs in an Open Key*
Jan Englis Leary — *Skating on the Vertical*
Marjorie Maddox — *What She Was Saying*
William Marquess — *Boom-shacka-lacka*
Gary Miller — *Museum of the Americas*
Jennifer Anne Moses — *Visiting Hours*
Martin Ott — *Interrogations*
Jack Pulaski — *Love's Labours*
Charles Rafferty — *Saturday Night at Magellan's*
Ron Savage — *What We Do For Love*
Fred Skolnik— *Americans and Other Stories*
Lynn Sloan — *This Far Is Not Far Enough*
L.E. Smith — *Views Cost Extra*
Caitlin Hamilton Summie — *To Lay To Rest Our Ghosts*
Susan Thomas — *Among Angelic Orders*
Tom Walker — *Signed Confessions*
Silas Dent Zobal — *The Inconvenience of the Wings*

Odd Birds

William Benton — *Eye Contact*
Micheal Breiner — *the way none of this happened*
J. C. Ellefson — *Under the Influence*
David Ross Gunn — *Cautionary Chronicles*
Andrei Guriuanu and Teknari — *The Darkest City*
Gail Holst-Warhaft — *The Fall of Athens*
Roger Leboitz — *A Guide to the Western Slopes and the Outlying Area*
dug Nap— *Artsy Fartsy*
Delia Bell Robinson — *A Shirtwaist Story*

Peter Schumann — *Bread & Sentences*
Peter Schumann — *Charlotte Salomon*
Peter Schumann — *Faust 3*
Peter Schumann — *Planet Kasper, Volumes One and Two*
Peter Schumann — *We*

Plays
Stephen Goldberg — *Screwed and Other Plays*
Michele Markarian — *Unborn Children of America*

Essays
Robert Sommer — *Losing Francis*